Everything

Everything

All the Things: part three

K. A. LAST

www.kalastbooks.com.au

K. A. Last
kalast@kalastbooks.com.au
www.kalastbooks.com.au

ISBN: 978-0-6480257-5-7

Formatting and cover design by KILA Designs
www.kiladesigns.com.au
Cover images: ©bigstockphoto.com

Editing by Lauren Clarke Editing
www.laurenclarkeediting.com

For KSS. Just do it!

Contents

A little bit more   1
My everything   12
So broken   23
It will come true   37
What *is* the point?   49
So hard   63
That stupid game   75
Thick and fast   90
My escape   102
Together again?   111
My fight   125
Coming home   138
Our future starts now   153

A little bit more

hat do I do?

How do I deal with this?

How do I deal when I've just been told the boy I love has had a life-threatening accident and is in the hospital?

I stare at my parents, clutching my purse to my chest. My phone inside vibrates through the fabric. I look at my hands and frown. A text message.

Maybe it's Levi.

But he's been in an accident.

Accident?

What kind of accident? Did he fall over?

I turn and fumble with the handle on the front door.

"Katie," Dad says. "Honey."

But I have the door open. I race down the steps and run to Levi's house, stepping through the garden bed

that borders our two properties.

Where is his car?

He told me he'd be home.

Was he driving? Was he drinking?

No. He said he wouldn't do that anymore.

What the hell is happening?

"Katie," Mum calls.

I reach the steps to Levi's veranda and take them in two bounds. I pound on the front door. My purse vibrates again and I fumble with the zipper as I try to get it open. My fingers shake and I can't get them to do what I want them to.

Finally, I get my phone out.

Karen: have u heard?

Karen: Katie? Call me!!!

Karen: Coming over now

The door to Levi's house opens before I can type a reply.

"What happened to Levi?" I blurt.

Yvonne presses her lips together, then looks over my shoulder. I glance behind me as Mum puts her foot on the bottom step.

"I'm sorry. Katie didn't give me a chance to tell her the details," Mum says.

"What details?" I look back at Yvonne.

She wrings her hands together. "Levi was in an accident."

"I know!" I shout.

"Katie." Mum puts her hand on my arm.

A tear slips down Yvonne's cheek. "I came home to get some things. I'm going back to the hospital soon. Maybe—"

"Tell me what happened, please." My palms go sweaty.

This can't be happening. "Is he okay? He told me he'd be here when I got home." Panic rises into my chest and I feel sick, like I'm about to vomit.

"Levi ..." Yvonne presses her lips together again, and folds her arms around herself. "He's ... in a coma. The doctors say he should recover."

I draw in a sharp breath. "Coma? *Should* recover?" I turn to Mum. "What ...?"

"Honey, you need to come home." She takes my hand and pulls me away. "I'm sorry, Yvonne. I'll tell her everything when we get inside."

I fight to free myself from Mum's grasp. "Tell me what?"

Karen pulls up at the kerb, and she's out of the car faster than I've ever seen her move. Her face is streaked with tears.

"Jess," she yells, stumbling across the lawn. "We have to go and see Jess."

Dad intercepts Karen in the driveway. He grabs her arms gently and tries to hug her. Karen struggles at first, but then she lets him hold her. I stop struggling as well, and let Mum guide me back down from Levi's veranda onto the path.

Levi is in the hospital.

Is Jessica as well?

Tears sting my eyes. I don't really know what's going on, but it's obviously bad. The fortune teller told me I needed to be prepared for something tragic. Well, I'm not prepared, and that stuff is all a bunch of bull. It's not supposed to be true. But an accident is a tragedy, and from the way all the adults look, it isn't good.

The front door to Levi's house clicks closed behind

me. Karen's parents pull into our driveway and get out of their car.

"I'm sorry," Karen's mum, Rebecca, calls. "Karen took off, and we assumed she'd come here."

"I think we should get the girls inside." Mums leads me over to our yard.

Dad nods, and passes Karen over to Rebecca. I walk numbly towards our front door. Karen buries her face into her mum's neck and sobs as she walks. I have no idea why she's so upset, but the sound makes me want to cry, too. I take a breath and hold back the tears.

Mum opens our front door and ushers everyone in. Rebecca is still hugging Karen, a grim expression marring her usually beautiful features. Karen's dad, Oliver, wraps both his girls in his big arms. Dad gently guides me until I'm sitting on the lounge. I drop my phone and purse onto the cushion.

"We're really sorry, honey," he says. "Levi is in the hospital, like we said, and he's in a pretty bad way, but there's more." He pauses, and exchanges a quick glance with Mum.

She continues, "Josephine was in the accident as well."

I let out a long breath. "But Jess is okay?" I glance at Karen.

"Not exactly," Mum says. "Josephine ... she didn't make it."

I suck in a sharp gasp. "What? What do you ... She died?" I shake my head. "No!"

I thought Josephine was a bitch, but I never wanted her to die. *Jessica*. Oh no, she must be crushed. She loves her sister, even if they fight more than they get along.

"No!" I say again, my voice too loud in my ears.

The room is quiet except for Karen's sniffles. I close my eyes, and put my face in my hands. A tear squeezes its way onto my cheek. This isn't happening. Yesterday, everything was perfect.

My heart strains at the thought of Levi lying in a hospital bed. *In a coma.* Can he hear anyone? Would he know me if I went to see him? I want to go and see him.

But Josephine.

Jessica.

Her sister is dead.

She'll need her friends.

"Jess … can we go see her?" I ask through my splayed fingers.

Karen pulls away from her parents' embrace and rubs her eyes.

"Yes, of course. Daniel is already over there," Mum says.

I look up. "When did this happen? *What* happened?" I squeeze my eyes closed again. What was Levi doing with Josephine?

"Last night," Dad says. "Josie … the police don't know exactly what happened yet. Levi can't … They can only go by the evidence at the accident scene. Levi's car hit Josie's directly on the driver's side. She … He's very lucky to be alive."

"They were in separate cars?" I ask. "Was there anyone else …?" I stare at Dad.

"No one else was involved," Mum says.

"Jess." I jump up from the lounge. "I need to see her."

Mum and Dad exchange a glance.

"Don't be too long," Mum says. "Jess will probably be tired. Bridget said she's been quite distraught."

Karen sniffles, and stares at me with wide eyes. Her face blurs through my tears, and I blink them away then go to the front door. Karen follows, and as we reach the bottom of my front steps, she slips her hand into mine. We walk down the street to Jessica's house in silence. I don't look back, but I get the feeling all of our parents are standing on the veranda watching us.

When we reach Jessica's front door, I raise my hand to knock and Karen releases her grip on me, hugging herself. After one of the longest minutes of my life, I go to knock again, but the door opens and Jessica's mum, Bridget, peers out. Her eyes are red and puffy, and she looks much older than her almost fifty years. She doesn't really look at us. It's as if she's looking through us.

"Come in, girls." Bridget turns away from the open door, and we follow her into the house. "Jess is in her room," she adds.

Karen and I exchange a glance

"I'm really sorry," I say, because what else do you say to someone who has lost their daughter?

Bridget nods before walking through to the kitchen.

Karen sets her foot on the top step and walks down the stairs. I follow her to Jessica's bedroom where we find her lying on her bed facing the wall. My brother sits in a chair at Jessica's desk, leaning forward with his elbows resting on his thighs.

What is he doing here? Jessica had a crush on him years ago, but I didn't think they were friends. I frown, and he stands. Karen and I hover in the doorway.

Daniel comes over to us and whispers, "I think she's sleeping."

Karen moves to sit on the end of the bed, and stares at our friend. I want to hug them, and Daniel. I want to hug all of them, and tell them how much I love them, because they could be gone at any moment. Like Josephine.

It's as if Daniel reads my mind. He puts his arms out and I step into them, pressing my face into his chest. He wraps me up in a brotherly hug, and rests his chin on the top of my head.

"How's she doing?" I ask, my voice muffled in Daniel's chest.

"Not so good," he says.

"What are you …?" I take a breath. "You and …?" I pull away and look up at my brother.

He shrugs. "You weren't here. She needed someone."

I frown, and look from my brother to my sleeping friend. Karen has her hand resting on Jessica's arm. "Is there …?"

"Katie, I'm just trying to help."

"Why didn't you call me?"

Daniel takes a deep breath. "We wanted you and Karen to get home safely. We didn't want you both worrying, and rushing to get back here."

I want to ask if he's seen Levi, but why would he have? He probably hasn't had time to go to the hospital. And Jessica might hear me. I'm still not sure exactly what happened. I don't want to upset her. She may not want to hear Levi's name.

"We can talk more when you get home," Daniel says, and I love that he knows me so well and can guess what

I'm thinking. He gives me another hug.

"See you soon," I say when he pulls away and moves towards the door.

Daniel gives me a closed-lipped smile. "I'll take you to the hospital later if you like."

"Maybe tomorrow," I say. If Levi is in a coma, his family might want to spend time with him first.

And right now, Jessica needs me.

Daniel gently closes the door on his way out.

Karen sniffles, and I take a few steps towards the bed and my friends. Hot tears prick my eyes, but I hold them in. I don't want to cry in front of Jessica.

When I reach the bed, Karen shuffles along a bit and I lie down beside Jessica. She stirs, and when I drape my arm over her and find her hand, she squeezes it tightly.

"I'm so sorry," I whisper.

Karen leans over and wraps her arms around both of us. Her fringe tickles my cheek. I prop myself up on my elbow and stroke Jessica's hair. She blinks, then closes her eyes so tight they crease at the corners. A tear slips out and rolls down onto her nose. Her body shakes under my embrace, and I grip her tighter. Karen tightens her hug as well. I know in that moment that we're holding Jessica together.

The door creaks as someone opens it, but none of us move.

The bed dips and Stacey crawls up it so she can lie between Jessica and the wall. She faces her, and her lips curl into a small smile.

"Hey you," Stacey says.

Karen and I stay how we are, me hugging Jessica,

and Karen hugging both of us.

Jessica swipes at her cheek with her free hand. "Hey," she whispers.

Stacey plays with the ends of Jessica's blonde strands, twisting them around her finger. She glances up at me and presses her lips together. What are we supposed to do now? How can we help Jessica? There's nothing we can do.

I feel helpless.

But that's nothing compared to how Jessica must feel.

My heart breaks for her, and I squeeze my eyes closed. Karen takes a deep breath behind me, and Stacey puts her hand over mine, the one that's holding Jessica's.

The four of us lie here on Jessica's bed, a bundle of messed up emotions with no idea how to fix what's broken.

"It's all my fault," Jessica whispers, and I raise my head a little, looking at Stacey with my mouth open.

"Oh no, Jess. It's not your fault," Stacey says, raising her eyebrows at me.

"Yes, it is." Jessica buries her face in the mattress.

"It was an accident." I stroke her hair again. "Just an accident."

"All my fault," Jessica says, her words muffled by the sheets on the bed.

She screams into the mattress, her body going rigid beside me.

Stacey's eyes widen. Karen lets go of us, and I prop myself up, putting my hand on Jessica's arm.

She screams again, balling the sheets in her fists.

"It's okay," Stacey says. "Everything will be okay."

"Nooooooo," Jessica wails. "Nothing is okay. I did this.

It's my fault. I did this, Josie. Oh my God, Josie!"

I jump up, my hands shaking. A mix of fear, pain, and heartache course through me, making my insides go cold. Stacey tries to hold Jessica, but she kicks and lashes out. Not really at Stacey, it seems, but at the world. Stacey gets off the bed, and the three of us stand and stare at our friend.

"It's not your fault, Jess." Tears burn tracks down my cheeks because I can't hold them in anymore.

"I killed her," Jessica yells. "It's my fault … all my fault."

"What do we do?" Karen whispers.

Stacey kneels beside the bed and murmurs to Jessica, her voice so low I can't make out her words.

Jessica calms a little, then rolls onto her stomach, and presses her face into her pillow. "Josie," she whispers. "Josie, Josie, Josie."

I take a step towards the bed and kneel down beside Stacey, laying my cheek on the mattress so my face is close to Jessica's. She's still whispering her sister's name.

"We're here for you," I whisper back. "Always."

Jessica angles her head until she's facing me. I offer her a small smile, and brush her matted hair away from her eyes.

"Where's Josie?" Jessica asks.

Oh, Jess.

"Shhh." I tuck her hair behind her ear.

"Josie," Jessica says again.

"It's all right," I say. "Close your eyes."

"Can I see Josie?" Jessica blinks, and teardrops bead on the ends of her eyelashes.

Karen kneels on the other side of Stacey. Stacey rubs Jessica's arm, and Karen strokes her back.

"I'm sure you can see her any time you like," I say. "All you have to do is close your eyes."

Jessica calls her sister's name another five times, and with each one of my friend's breaths, my heart breaks a little bit more.

2

My everything

Jessica fell asleep after her outburst, so Karen and I left Stacey with her. Karen's parents took her home, and Mum and Dad wanted to 'talk' but talking was the last thing on my mind. I went to bed early, and had a restless sleep because all I could think about was Josephine, and the fact that Levi is lying in a hospital bed, in a coma, and won't be climbing in my window.

Now, it's mid-morning and I'm sitting at the kitchen counter, picking at a piece of toast, because not only did I not sleep very well, but I have no appetite.

"Visiting hours for ICU start soon," Mum says. "Want me to drive you?"

"Daniel said he'd take me."

"You don't want your dad and me to come?" Mum sets her cup of coffee on the bench.

I shake my head. "No. It's okay."

Mum comes to my side of the counter and slides onto the stool beside me. She puts an arm around my shoulders, pulling me close. "You should try and prepare yourself, okay? I won't lie. It's not nice. But when I saw Levi, he'd just been brought in. Mark was at work, so I drove Yvonne to the hospital not long after it happened. She was … distraught." Mum pushes my hair away from my face. "Today will be different though. I'm sure they're taking good care of him."

I rest my head on Mum's shoulder and stare at my hands, picking my fingernails. "I'm scared," I whisper.

"I know." Mum kisses my temple. "Sure you don't want us to come?"

"I'm sure."

"Okay." She gets up and takes her coffee cup to the sink. "I'll call Yvonne and let her know you're coming. She'll need to clear it with the hospital."

I nod, then put my forehead on the counter and stare at the little flecks in the laminate surface. I let my eyes relax, and it looks as if I'm surrounded by black stars in a daytime galaxy.

"Katie," Daniel says a few minutes later.

I roll my head to the side to look in the direction of his voice. He has his cheek resting on the counter and is staring at me.

"What?" I ask.

"You ready to go to the hospital?"

"What if I say no? What if I say I'm sitting here waiting to wake up from this nightmare?"

"I'd tell you visiting hours start at eleven-thirty, and

your ride is leaving in five minutes." He smiles.

"I'm not dreaming?" I close my eyes.

Daniel doesn't answer, and I don't open my eyes. I feel him move beside me. He covers my hand with his and squeezes. "Come on."

I sigh and get up from the stool, go to my room, and quickly brush my hair. I don't bother with my contacts today. Levi won't see me anyway. I grab my purse and phone, and go outside. My brother is already waiting in the car.

He turns the key in the ignition as I slide into the front passenger seat. I grip my purse in my lap to stop my fingers trembling, and chew my bottom lip.

Daniel pulls onto the street, and we head towards the highway. He turns the music up, and I'm grateful he doesn't try to talk to me.

I think about Levi as we drive. What will he look like? Will he have tubes coming out of him? Are his injuries bad? They must be if he's in a coma. But maybe it's a precaution. I've heard of doctors putting people in comas on purpose.

"Did you hear me?" Daniel says.

"Huh?" I turn towards my brother.

He glances at me before making a left-hand turn into the street the hospital is on. "Do you want me to come in with you?" He finds a park on the street and pulls over.

I bite my lip again. Yes, I want him to come with me. I'm not sure I can walk in there on my own.

"Do you ... want to come in?" I ask.

"I want to make sure you're okay."

"Then yes," I say. "Please come with me."

"Okay." Daniel nods. "Let's do this." He opens his door and gets out.

I hesitate, fiddling with the zipper on my purse. I'm not sure I can get out of the car. I can't do this. I don't want to face what's inside the hospital.

My door opens, and Daniel looks down at me. He doesn't say anything. He just reaches out and takes my hand, gently pulling me from the car.

"I can't do this," I whisper.

"Yes, you can." He closes my door and leads me across the street.

I hesitate at the front doors to the hospital. Daniel gives my hand a gentle tug, and I follow him through to the cool interior of the reception area.

"We're here to see Levi White," Daniel says to the nurse behind the desk.

"One minute." She turns to her computer and taps at the keyboard. "He's in ICU. Are you family?"

I press my lips together and shake my head, blinking to hold back my tears.

"We're neighbours," Daniel says.

"I'm sorry, family members only." The nurse smiles with her lips closed.

I tuck my purse under my arm and wring my hands together. My breath hitches. Daniel puts an arm around my shoulders, and I lean into him.

"Our mum was calling Yvonne White to let her know we were coming," Daniel says. "Can you call the ward and ask if we can go in? Please? We're Daniel and Katie Sullivan."

The nurse frowns, but she picks up the phone anyway.

I close my eyes and wait, listening to the beat of Daniel's heart.

"Yes, this is front desk," the nurse says. "I have some people here to see Levi White. Is there approval for non-family members?"

I open my eyes and stand up straighter.

The nurse nods. "Yes. Daniel and Katie … okay." She places the phone receiver back in the cradle and smiles at us. "You may go in. Along the hall to the end, then turn right. Use the phone on the left wall to request access, then make sure you wash your hands before you go in."

"Thank you," I say.

Daniel guides me away, and we follow the nurse's directions to the ICU.

He lifts the phone receiver. "Hi, we're here to see Levi White."

I don't hear what's said on the other end, but my brother nods and hangs up the phone. We scrub our hands with warm soapy water in the small sink on the wall, then wait.

The automatic doors open, and another nurse greets us with a smile. "Daniel and Katie? Levi is in room seven."

We follow her into the ward, and past another reception desk. I can't help looking into the rooms. There are so many machines and tubes. Lots of beeping. My chest tightens because I have no idea what to expect, or how Levi will look.

The nurse stops outside room seven. The curtains are drawn most of the way across the large glass window in the wall. She taps lightly on the door before opening it wide enough to put her head through.

"Daniel and Katie are here," she says.

I step up to the window and look through the gap in the curtains. Yvonne gets to her feet from a chair beside Levi's bed. I fix my gaze on her, because I'm not sure I can cope with looking at anything else. The other details of the room become a fuzzy blur.

Yvonne takes the few steps to the door, and I blink, readjusting my focus as I finally look at Levi. My breath hitches, and a tear splashes onto my cheek.

There's a big tube coming out of his mouth, leading to a machine beside the head of the bed. His face is covered in an angry red graze. A bandage comes out from under his hospital gown and over his left shoulder. Wires extend from the creases of his elbows and the backs of his hands, draping over the sides of the bed where they're hooked up to several more beeping machines.

I step back from the window. Panic makes my blood cold, and I shake. Daniel puts his hands on my shoulders from behind. "Calm down," he whispers in my ear.

"Katie," Yvonne says. The nurse holds the door open for her as she comes out of the room. "Do you and Daniel want to go in?"

I tear my gaze away from the window and stare at her. Her eyes are redder than they were when I saw her yesterday. I rub my arms to try and ward off the cold feeling inside me. Then I nod.

"Only two visitors at a time," the nurse says when Daniel and I reach the door.

"I'll go and get a coffee," Yvonne says.

Before I can protest and tell her she can go back in

with Daniel, she's already walking down the hall. Daniel nudges me gently into the room. He sits in a chair against the wall, leaving the one beside the bed empty. I stop a couple of metres away from Levi. I can't sit near him yet. I need more time to process everything.

The nurse quickly checks something on one of the machines, and makes a note on the chart hanging from the end of the bed.

"Can he hear us?" I ask, clutching my purse tightly.

"We don't really know," the nurse says. "He's in an induced coma."

"How … how long for?" I ask.

The nurse comes over and puts a hand on my arm. "Levi has a broken collarbone, three broken ribs, and a punctured lung … as well as other internal injuries. He had surgery following his accident, and his pain would have been excessive, so he needed help to heal. There's no way to know exactly how long he'll be under, but the doctors will monitor him and decide when to bring him out."

I take a step towards the bed. "Can I … hold his hand?"

"Of course," the nurse says. "Just pretend I'm not here. I'll be in and out on a regular basis, but if I'm not here and you need anything, press the green button on the wall beside the bed." She smiles and busies herself checking Levi's drip line.

I glance at Daniel, unsure what to do, then I look back at Levi. I have so many things to say to him, but can he even hear me? What if it all falls on deaf ears? Am I better off just going home? What good am I to him anyway?

"I reckon he can hear us," Daniel says, as if he can read my mind. He props his elbow on the armrest of the chair. "I'll go find us a drink while you have a chat." He gets up and gives me a quick kiss on the forehead on his way to the door. "Back soon."

I wait for what feels like a full minute after Daniel leaves, then I sit in the chair beside the bed, setting my purse and phone in my lap. The railing is up, and I drag the chair a little closer. I'm not sure how to hold his hand. There are so many wires and tubes, and he has a pulse monitor on his index finger. I don't want to bump anything, or hurt him, so I sit and stare at him for a few heartbeats.

If I didn't know it was Levi lying in this bed, then I'm not sure I would recognise him. The tube used to intubate him is thick, and strapped to his head. The air being pushed in and out of his lungs makes a haunting sound. His face is red, and I guess that it's from the airbag in the car, but I really don't know. The rest of his body is covered by a white hospital gown, and going by the scratches and bruises on his arms, it's probably a good thing.

I reach through the bars and rest my elbows on the side of the bed. Carefully, I touch the back of his hand with my fingertips. His skin is cool. Tears well in my eyes, and I lean my forehead against the metal bedrail.

"Hey, Levi. It's me. Katie." I swallow, but it's hard because my mouth is dry. "I want you to know I'm mad at you again. You said you'd be there when I got home." I press my palm to the back of his hand and curl my fingers around it. "You weren't there." The tears come faster, and I choke back a sob. "You said you'd be there."

I blink, but more tears fall, wetting my cheeks and making my eyes burn. I slip my other fingers under Levi's so I'm cupping his hand with both of mine. The machines beep around us in time with my heartbeats, and I count to fifty before I'm able to talk again.

"But I also want to tell you … I forgive you." I take a deep breath, sit up straight in the chair, and stare at Levi's face. If only I could will him to open his eyes and see me. "You hurt me, more than once, and I can't pretend to understand why you did everything you did, but I can understand what my heart feels. I forgive you for everything. I love you. I have always loved you, and we've been through too much for either of us to give up now." My voice shakes, and I have to stop as more tears come. "You're going to get better."

The door opens behind me, and Daniel comes to my side. He puts a hand on my shoulder. "I brought you a cup of tea."

I reluctantly let go of Levi's hand and take the steaming cup from Daniel. "Thanks." I offer my brother a half-smile. "I wish I could go back to the last time I saw him." I take a sip of my tea. "Telling him I love him now doesn't seem to count."

"I think it does," Daniel says.

I smile and hope Daniel is right.

We're quiet for a few minutes, sipping our drinks and listening to the ventilator and the beeping machines. My phone buzzes in my lap, and I look down at the lit up screen.

Karen: How ru 2day?

I pick up the phone and unlock it, pressing the message icon.

Me: At hospital

Karen: How's Levi?

Me: Alive

I put my phone away, sit back in the chair, and glance towards the door. Yvonne is at the window, looking into the room through the gap in the curtains. She smiles at me, but it doesn't reach her eyes.

A knock sounds at the door and the nurse comes in. She fusses about, checking some readings on the monitors. Then she opens the curtains on the window.

Mark stands beside Yvonne, towering over her, a frown furrowing his brow. She has one arm wrapped around herself, and her other hand covers her mouth. Her eyes glisten under the hospital lighting.

"Maybe we should go," I say, turning back to look at Levi.

"You don't want to stay longer?" Daniel asks.

"I think they want to spend time with him." I nod towards the window behind my brother.

He glances over his shoulder. "Okay. Time to say goodbye."

"Goodbye is too final," I say, getting up from my seat beside the bed.

I lean over the bedrail and concentrate on Levi's face. His eyelids are purple, and I want them to open so badly so I can look at him, but all I get is the tiny ripple of his eyes moving underneath. I hope he's dreaming about me. About us.

His hand is still cool when I slip my fingers around it and squeeze gently. "I'll see you soon," I whisper.

I take a couple of steps towards the door. When I reach it, I can't help looking back, and a wave of emotion hits me all over again. It crashes into my heart, drowning it in sorrow, and pain. My breath catches in my throat. I'm somehow shocked even more now at the sight of Levi lying broken in his hospital bed than I was when I first entered the room.

How do I fix him?

How do I put his pieces back together again? I have to, because Levi is *my* missing piece. He's all the things that make me whole.

He's my everything.

So broken

My phone rings, buzzing against the surface of my desk, for what seems like the millionth time. I lie on my bed, staring at it, waiting for it to shut up. It stops, and I close my eyes.

The buzzing starts again.

I blink a few times, then reach out and snatch my phone up.

Karen's name flashes on the screen.

I don't want to answer it, because she'll ask me about Levi, and I'm not sure I'll be able to talk about him without bursting into tears.

The phone stops again, and I roll onto my back to stare at my ceiling. It's mid-morning, so my glow-in-the-dark stars are dormant.

My phone rings again.

I lift my arm and stare at the screen. Karen is persistent.

I sigh, and press the answer icon. "Hello."

"Oh my God, why won't you pick up your phone?" Karen asks.

"I answered it," I say. "I'm talking to you now."

"Come on, Katie. You've been moping in your room for three days. I'm coming to pick you up."

"No," I say, but she's already hung up.

And I haven't been in my room *all* that time.

I've been to see Jessica a couple of times—as hard as it was.

I've also been to the hospital to see Levi every day.

The first time I saw him was traumatic. He had so many tubes and wires sticking out of him. It was scary, and unreal, and emotionally draining. But I know what to expect now, so it's getting a little easier.

Ten minutes later, a car pulls up outside, and I take a deep breath. Karen will be in my room any second, trying to cheer me up. I love her, and that she wants to do that, but I'm not sure I have the energy today.

"Katie," Daniel calls from downstairs. "Karen's here."

"In my room," I say.

A few moments later, Karen pushes my door open and comes to sit on the bed. She looks a lot better than she did the day we got home from Surfers Paradise. I've never seen her so upset before, but today it's as if she's back to her old self. I guess we all cope in our own way, but I hope she's not bottling stuff up.

"You okay?" I ask.

"Today is a new day." She smiles. "We should make the most of it. You never know when your time will be up."

I pinch the bridge of my nose. "Our world fell apart three days ago."

"We need hot chocolate." Karen grabs my hands and pulls me to sitting. "Hot chocolate fixes everything."

"I don't want to go out," I whine.

"Well, I do." She stands, and pulls my arms again, and I give in and get up, too. "Ten minutes and I want you in the car. You can't go out in your PJs."

I stare at Karen's back as she leaves my room. It looks like she's not taking no for an answer, so I pull on a pair of shorts and a clean top. I go to the bathroom and give my face a quick wash, then run my fingers through my hair and put my glasses on. Back in my room, I grab my tote and shove my phone, purse, journal, and a pen inside.

"Daniel? I'm going out," I say on my way down the stairs.

"Have fun." He waves at me from the lounge.

Karen smiles as I hop in the car. She starts the engine, then grips the steering wheel and pulls out into the street.

"Have you been to see Jess?" I ask when we turn onto the highway.

"Not since the other day," Karen says. "You?"

"Yeah." I stare at my hands. "There's no change. If anything she seems … more broken. She has Stacey, so maybe she can help her? I'm not sure me being there has been good for her. I think I'm too close to Levi, and he's probably not her favourite person right now."

"It would be hard. Has she talked about him?" Karen says.

I shrug. "She doesn't talk much."

"Do you blame Levi for what happened?" Karen stares straight ahead.

I study the profile of her face. "We don't know the details. And I haven't heard his side of the story, so how can I?"

We drive for a bit before Karen breaks our silence. "Are you going to see him today?"

I fiddle with the handle of my tote bag. "I've been to see him every day since ..."

Karen turns into the shopping centre car park. "Want me to come with?"

"Do you want to see him? We'll have to get Yvonne to authorise it though. The hospital has said family only. We could go later this afternoon."

Karen swings the car into an empty space and kills the engine. She turns in her seat to face me. "Is it ... hard to, you know. See him?"

If I had been a good friend and answered my phone, then I would have told Karen all this stuff already. But I didn't want to talk about it, and I still don't. I squeeze my eyes closed, but then I open them again because my thoughts immediately fill with images of Levi in his hospital bed.

"He's in a coma, so yeah. It's hard. He's pretty bad."

"Oh, Katie, I'm so sorry." Karen leans over and hugs me.

She presses her hands into my back, and I bury my face in her neck. I don't want to cry. Crying doesn't fix anything. But I can't hold it in. And I don't want to be strong. I want to go home and crawl into bed and forget about the world.

"Come on," Karen says. "Hot chocolate?"

I nod and we get out of the car, walking through the shopping centre and into the mall. We order our usual, but instead of sitting in we decide to wander through the shops while we drink. It feels good to be out walking around, but my heart is heavy, and every time I think my mind has taken a break from picturing Levi fighting for his life, it reminds me what's happened all over again.

Why can't I switch off for a few minutes? I'm going crazy.

"I want to go home," I say to Karen.

She's looking in the window of a jewellery store. "Okay."

She links her arm with mine, and we make our way through the lunch crowd in the shopping centre, back towards the car. We drive home with the windows down and the music up, only I don't sing along like I often do. I lean against the window frame and let the wind blow my hair away from my face, pretending that it's also blowing away the pain.

Karen leans over and turns the music down. "Have you driven past where … you know? It happened?" she asks when we turn off the highway.

I bite my lip. "You mean the accident site?" I shake my head. "No."

Karen grips the steering wheel. "Want to? I hear there's a great tribute going on."

"Sure, I guess." But I'm not sure. Do I want to see the place where the sister of one of my closest friends died? The place where Levi's life was changed in an instant?

Karen turns onto a backstreet we don't usually take. She waits at the stop sign before driving through the intersection and parking at the kerb. The telegraph pole on the corner is an explosion of colour. Karen gets out, and I slowly follow, squinting against the sunlight.

The pole is covered with flowers, pieces of paper, and photos. In the middle of it all is a white cross with a photo of Josephine and her name on it. There are more flowers on the ground surrounding the pole.

Emptiness fills my stomach, because I don't have anything to offer Josephine. I haven't written her a card, or brought her anything. I should have brought her something.

"Can we go?" I turn away and head to the car before Karen can answer.

She doesn't object, and by the time we pull into my driveway, everything hurts more than it did before.

"You've got mail," Karen says before getting out of the car.

I glance over at our letterbox. A few rolled up white envelopes stick out from the front. I take a deep breath and get out of the car, too. My uni letters are probably in there somewhere, they should be arriving soon, but right now I'm not all that interested. How can I think about my future when Josephine doesn't have one, and Levi might not have one either?

We might not have one together.

I go to the mailbox and grab everything that's inside, flipping through the envelopes, pieces of paper, and brochures on the way to the house. Karen holds the bundle while I unlock the front door.

"Hey, you've got uni letters." Karen waves some of the envelopes in the air. "My money says they're all acceptances."

"I don't really care at the moment." I close the door

behind us and walk through to the kitchen.

"But this will take your mind off things." Karen drops the mail onto the bench.

I stare at the envelopes and shake my head. "I'll open them later."

"Open what later?" Mum comes through into the kitchen, dumping her handbag and keys onto the bench.

"Sorry, Sonja. I parked in the driveway," Karen says.

Mum smiles. "Don't be. There's plenty of room on the street."

"You're home early," I say.

"I wanted to check on you." She kisses me on the temple, then goes to boil the kettle.

"I'm fine, Mum. Karen took me for hot chocolate."

"Katie has university letters," Karen says.

I shoot her dagger eyes.

Mum gets her coffee cup down from the cupboard. "Have you opened them?"

"No," I say. "And I'm not going to."

"Why not?" Mum spoons coffee into her cup and pours in the boiling water.

"Because I'm not in the mood." I stare down at the letters, then move them so I can see the university logos. The specific one I'm waiting for isn't there, but another catches my eye.

I pick up the envelope, and look at the front. The Art Express logo is printed in the upper left-hand corner.

Karen peers over my shoulder. "Oh my God, open it!"

A bolt of excitement hits me, and I slip my finger under the edge to rip the paper open. I pull the letter out and unfold it, quickly scanning the words.

"What does it say?" Mum asks.

"What does what say?" Daniel looks over my other shoulder.

"Where did you come from?" I look up at him.

"Through the door." He glances over his shoulder then back at me.

"Katie!" Karen says. "What the hell does it say?"

I scan the words again to find the most important part. "Your artwork, *Wearable Wisdom*, has been selected for the upcoming Art Express exhibition. Another letter will follow shortly with instructions on how to submit your work."

"That's great news," Mum says. "I'm so proud of you." But there's something about her tone that suggests she's only saying that because she has to.

"Congrats, little sis." Daniel play-punches my arm.

Mum picks up the uni letters. "Now you can open these."

I bite my lip and stare at her hand, shaking my head. It's one thing to get accepted into an art exhibition, but it's another to have to look at something that's going to decide the next four years of my life.

"Not yet," I say.

"Katie, I want you to open them." Mum pushes the paper towards me.

"No." I back away.

Mum frowns, picking the letters up. "I can open them for you."

"No!" I say again, lunging forward and snatching them from her grasp.

"Katie! What is wrong with you?" Mum says.

I clutch the envelopes to my chest. "The past few days

have been a nightmare. Sorry if I don't want to look at something that could determine my entire future. Levi might not even have a future, so how can I think about mine?"

Mum's eyes widen, and she stares at me.

I turn and run outside, still holding the letters to my chest. I have to resist the urge to rip them up and throw them straight in the recycling bin. How can she want me to open them now? Can't I have a little while to fully process everything that's happened?

I stand on the lawn and look at the bougainvillea, and a fresh wave of grief hits me.

A door slams, and I look over to Levi's veranda. Yvonne comes out with hurried steps, Mark hot on her heels.

"Come back here," he says.

Levi's mum turns at the top veranda step, her brow furrowed. "I'm going to the hospital, and you can't stop me."

"Don't use that tone with me." Mark grabs her wrist.

She tries to yank it away. "Let go! You're hurting me."

He pulls her closer to him and mumbles something, but I can't make out the words. I can only hear the low, menacing tone in his voice. Why are they fighting?

"Let go." Yvonne grimaces, and fights her husband to free his grip on her arm.

Her gaze flicks to me, and I stand as still as I can, clutching my uni letters. Mark stops pulling her and follows her line of sight. He lets her go, narrows his eyes at me, then goes back inside the house.

Yvonne presses her lips together, walking to her car with her eyes forward and her shoulders back. She starts the engine and pulls away from the kerb.

What is going on?

I never saw Levi's dad act like this when I was a kid. How long has he been treating his wife like this? How long has Levi been dealing with it, and I haven't known?

Karen bumps me with her shoulder, and I snap out of my shock.

"Did you see any of that?" I ask.

"Any of what?"

"Levi's parents. Something's going on, and it doesn't look good."

Karen moves so she's standing in front of me. "Something? What something?"

"He was being … He looked like he wanted to hit her."

"That's pretty heavy." Karen glances over her shoulder at Levi's house.

"Yvonne went to the hospital."

"You want to go now, too?" Karen turns back to me.

I nod. "I'll put these inside."

I run in and dump the uni letters on my desk, grabbing my tote on the way back out. I don't bother telling Mum where I'm going. I'm still upset that she tried to make me open my mail, and I'm sure she'll be able to figure it out.

Karen and I take the motorway to the hospital. I curl my fingers around the shape of my journal inside my tote bag. I've wanted to write in it ever since I found out about Josephine's death, and Levi ending up in hospital. But for some reason I can't. I figure if I take it places with me, the motivation might strike when I least expect it.

I take the small book out and hold it in my lap, running my finger over the smooth cover.

"You going to write in that?" Karen asks, turning into the hospital street.

"I don't know if I can," I say. "The past few days are filled with things I don't want to remember. If I write them down, they'll always be there."

"Everything will always be there no matter what." Karen parks the car on the street. "If you write it down, at least it will be out of your head, and you might be able to make more sense of it all."

"Maybe." I put my journal back in my bag.

We get out and cross the road to the hospital. This time I don't bother with reception, and we walk straight to the door of the ICU.

I pick up the phone on the wall. "Hi, this is Katie Sullivan. I'm here to see Levi White."

"Hi Katie," a nurse says, and I recognise her voice from the other day. "Are you by yourself?"

"I have a friend with me. Karen Mitchell. Can you ask Yvonne if Karen can come through, please?"

"One moment." There's some rustling at the end of the phone line. "Yes, Katie. Yvonne says that's fine."

"Thank you." I hang up the phone.

The automatic doors open as Karen and I finish washing out hands. I lead her to room seven, noticing that she looks into all the rooms as we pass, like I did that first time. At Levi's room, the curtain is fully open this time, so he's on display to the entire ward. I understand why the rooms are like this—it helps with monitoring the patients—but looking at him like he's in a fishbowl makes me sad.

Karen stands at the window. "He doesn't look too bad."

I stand beside her, and rest my hand on the window

frame. "His breathing tube is gone."

"They took it out this morning." Yvonne is on my other side, staring through the glass at her son, a takeaway coffee cup in her hand.

"Oh." I look her up and down quickly. She seems more composed now than when I saw her at home. "That's a good thing, right?"

She turns to me. "It means they're bringing him out of the coma. He's still heavily sedated, but he's breathing on his own, which is good, yes. You girls can go in." She smiles weakly.

Karen moves to the door, and I go to follow but stop and turn back to Levi's mum. "Is everything okay?"

"I'm sure everything will be fine. I'm just trying to focus on getting Levi better."

I press my lips together and nod, then go into the room with Karen.

"Can he ... hear us?" She fidgets with the bangle on her left wrist.

"I asked the same thing the first time I saw him." I drop my tote on the floor and sit in the chair beside the bed. "They said they don't really know, but talking to him can't hurt."

Karen comes closer. "Okay, um, so, Levi. I think you're an arse, and you've done some stupid stuff, but, you know. Don't die, please. Because then I'll have to put up with Katie. So, yeah."

I look up at Karen. She raises her eyebrows, and we both burst out laughing. My shoulders shake, and it feels good to let the emotion out. Tears run down my face and I swipe them away, but they keep coming until my laughter turns to sobs.

"Oh, Katie." Karen stands beside me and puts her arm around my shoulders.

I spurt another short laugh, then sniffle. "I hope he can hear us, because the other day I told him I love him."

Karen rubs my back. "I'll leave you two kids to talk."

I smile up at her and she leaves the room, standing with Yvonne on the other side of the window.

I turn back to Levi. "Hey, you."

He doesn't look as scary, now that the big tube is out of his mouth. His face is still quite bruised and chaffed, but he looks more like himself.

"I brought my journal with me." I reach down and take it and a pen out of my tote bag. "I haven't written in it yet. Not since … you know." I grip the edge of the small book and hold it in my lap. "It's hard to process everything that's happened. I'm not sure I can write it down in words, because my brain is so full of stuff, and it feels all mixed up." I pause, and slip one hand through the bedrail to hold Levi's. He's a little warmer today. "Karen seems to think if I write everything down, it might help me cope better."

I let go of his hand and open my journal, grasping the pen and pressing the nib to a fresh page. I write the date, then stop.

"But where do I start, Levi?"

I take a breath and write.

The day we left Surfers, Levi told me he would be there when I got home. I was so upset that he wasn't, because I was ready to tell him I forgive him.

Then I found out Levi had been in an accident which put him in intensive care, and killed Josie. Her death is terrible, and Jess is so broken over it, but I'm broken, too.

In a way, I'm also happy. Not because Josephine died, but because Levi lived. And while I don't know all of the details yet, I'm so happy that he's still here. Is that an awful way to think? Am I a bad person, because I'm so glad he lived when the sister of one of my close friends didn't?

I don't know how to deal with all the emotions, or how to put my thoughts in the right order. Levi is in a pretty bad way. They say he'll be fine, but it's hard to believe that when he can't even talk to me.

I stop and lean my forehead against the bedrail. Tears come again, and I close my journal. I can't write anymore. It's too hard, and my heart hurts because right now, even though I'm alive and Levi is fighting to live, we are both so broken.

4

It will come true

The past week has been hard. Daniel has been the best big brother ever, taking me to the hospital whenever I ask, even though staying at home in my bubble would have been the easier thing to do.

Now, it's the day of Josephine's funeral, and I have to face Josephine's family, and Levi and Josephine's friends. Is everyone angry with Levi? Do they think the accident was his fault? I haven't asked Mum and Dad any questions about the accident, and they haven't offered any more information.

I'm not sure I want to know the details.

Because I'm already hurting so bad.

I change slowly into a navy A-line dress with little cap sleeves. It's one of the nicest dresses I own, but I haven't worn it since Mason's funeral, which makes wearing it now even harder. The memories that go with it are painful.

In the bathroom I put my contacts in, and dust some powder over my face before sweeping gloss over my lips. I'm as ready as I'm ever going to be, so I grab my purse and head downstairs.

"Katie, can you take the paper recycling out?" Mum asks as I walk into the kitchen. She's dressed in a sleek black dress that stops at her knees, and is putting in black teardrop earrings.

"Sure." I set my purse down and grab the basket off the counter.

Mum stops and stares at me. "Oh, honey. You look so lovely in that dress."

"Thanks." I stare at the basket of paper in my hands.

"I haven't seen you wear it since—"

"Mason's funeral." I can't look at her or I'll cry, so I head outside to the bins at the side of the house.

With the basket tucked under my arm, I flip the lid of the bin open then rest the basket on the edge to tip it up. I stop halfway and stare at the newspaper sitting on top of all the other recyclable stuff inside. There are photos of Levi and Josephine on the front page. I stand there for a few moments, staring at it. Do I want to read it? Why have I not seen this yet? Are Mum and Dad hiding things like this from me? I set the basket on the ground, fish the newspaper out, and quickly scan the article.

LOCAL GIRL KILLED IN CAR ACCIDENT
Josephine Hart was killed when her Honda Civic was struck by a BMW late Friday night. Levi White, the driver of the BMW, is currently in a

critical but stable condition. Mandatory tests revealed both drivers were not under the influence, and police have ruled out speed as a factor. There were no witnesses. Evidence at the scene suggests Miss Hart failed to stop at the intersection for reasons unknown. Police are hopeful a future statement from Mr White will shed some light on what happened.

At least Levi hadn't been drinking. And everyone would know the intersection the article is referring to. Anyone who runs that stop sign is asking for trouble. I'm not sure why Mum and Dad don't want me to see this, because knowing Levi wasn't drunk has lifted a weight from my shoulders. But that weight crashes back down again, because Josephine is still dead. Me feeling better is not going to change that.

I toss the paper back in the bin, then dump the rest of the recycling on top.

Mum, Dad, and Daniel come out the front door. Dad takes the basket from me and puts it in the foyer.

Mum hands me my purse. "We have to go."

I take a deep breath, and we all pile into the car.

The local church is five minutes away, and when we arrive there's already a crowd of people milling around outside the doors.

"Why is everyone looking at their phone?" Daniel asks.

"HSC results release today," I say.

"Oh, I completely forgot," Mum says. "Katie, do you want to look at yours?"

"No." I glare at her. "Mum, we're at a funeral."

"We're still in the car. I'm sure you can take a couple of minutes."

I shake my head, open my mouth to say something but close it again, then get out. What is wrong with everyone? Josephine can't look at her results. Neither can Levi.

"Katie ..." Dad says when we're all out of the car.

"My results will still be there tomorrow." I glare at my parents before turning towards the church.

"You okay?" Daniel comes to my side.

"No. I'm not." I stomp away from him, towards Karen and Stacey who are standing on the edge of the crowd staring at their phone.

"Did you get your results?" Karen asks when I'm close enough to hear her.

My mouth drops open. "No. Have some respect. Put your phones away."

Karen and Stacey exchange a glance but do it anyway.

Veronica comes over to our little group. "Hey, Katie." She plays with the small black purse in her hands. "How are you?"

I sigh, because this is where I'm supposed to tell her I'm fine, but I'm far from it, and I'm tired of pretending. Then I remember that Josephine was one of Veronica's best friends, and Levi is still her friend, so I say exactly what I'm supposed to. "I'm okay. Thanks for asking. How about you? This must be hard."

Veronica offers me a weak smile. "I haven't been able to see Levi yet. None of us have. His mum won't let us into the ICU. Is he ...?"

"I think he's doing well," I say, surprised that Yvonne

let Daniel, Karen and I in, but not the others. "They brought him out of the coma, but he's on heavy painkillers. He hasn't been awake when I've been to see him."

Veronica nods, then angles her head towards the church. "I'm going in."

Most of the crowd has moved inside already, so Karen, Stacey, and I follow. We take the left-side aisle along the wall, and I notice Yvonne sitting in the very back row by herself. I can't see Levi's dad anywhere.

Karen, Stacey, and I move towards the front to see if we can sit near Jessica. She's in the front row with her parents, and we take the pew two rows back. Mum and Dad are across the aisle from us, but when Daniel spots me he moves to sit beside me. He gives my hand a gentle squeeze, and I think maybe I can get through the next few hours.

The service is emotional, and when Jessica gets up for the eulogy, I cry just as hard as she does. I'm so proud of her though, because she manages to get through it on her own. We stay until the hearse takes the coffin away.

Outside, Daniel hugs me, and I hold onto him as if he's the only thing keeping me on my feet.

"Want to go to the hospital?" he asks.

I nod into his chest.

"I can come with you," Karen says, rubbing my back. "I don't think I can handle the wake."

I pull out of Daniel's embrace. "I'd like to go see Levi by myself today."

"Okay." She tucks my hair behind my ear. "Stacey and I will look after Jess."

"Do you think she'll mind if I'm not there?"

"Why don't you ask her?" Daniel says.

I crane my neck to search for my friend. She's with her mum and dad, doing the rounds. Jessica's eyes are puffy and red. I walk over to her and touch her on the elbow. When she sees me her face crumples, and I take her into my arms and hold her while she cries.

"I'm so sorry." I grip her tightly.

"Are you coming this afternoon?" Jessica pulls away and searches my face.

I press my lips together. "I'd like to go and see Levi. They've taken him out of the coma. He might be awake." I pause, and Jessica stays quiet. "I can come if you'd like though?"

She shakes her head. "No, it's okay. He needs you."

"But you need me, too."

"I have Stacey." She glances at our friend. "And Karen. Levi needs you more than I do."

I hug her again, because no words I have will be able to take away her pain. "I'll call you later."

Daniel and I go home with Mum and Dad. I don't bother to change, but I do run inside to grab my journal. Then my brother and I head for the hospital.

"You right to get home?" Daniel says.

"Yeah. I'll call if I need you." I shut the car door and cross the street, making my way to the ICU.

A nurse lets me in, and I go to Levi's room, knocking gently on the door before going inside.

"There's no change," Yvonne says, getting up from the chair beside the bed. "I'll let you have some privacy."

"Thank you," I say.

Yvonne touches me on the arm on her way past. I

want to say more to her, but I don't know what, so I stay quiet. Once she has left, I sit in the chair and take out my journal.

"It's me again," I say to Levi, squeezing his hand. "They had Josie's funeral today, but your mum probably already told you. Jess did okay. Her eulogy was really beautiful." I go quiet for a minute.

"HSC results came out today as well. I haven't looked at mine. I'm not sure I want to. I don't think it's fair, you know, because you can't look at yours." I pause. "I was hoping we could look at them together." I squeeze his hand again, waiting for some sort of response, but there's nothing. All I can see is the steady rise and fall of Levi's chest as he breathes, and hear the constant beeping of the machines around us.

"I got some uni letters as well. I didn't tell you about those because I haven't opened them yet. Mum wants me to, but ... all of this I want to do with you. I thought I was going to come home from schoolies, and we were going to start a new chapter, one where we had a fresh page, and we could make our story whatever we wanted it to be." I rub circles on the back of Levi's hand with my thumb. "I also don't want to open them because the letter I've been hoping for the most hasn't come. I haven't told anyone but Karen I applied for a fine arts degree. Mum and Dad would freak out if I said I want to do something in the arts. They've always assumed I would do law, or become a doctor, but after seeing you like this, I don't think I could cope with that." I stare at Levi's face, searching for any sign that he can hear me. "I'm scared. If I tell them what I *really* want to do, they'll probably think I've completely wasted my scholarship."

I close my eyes and concentrate on the feeling of Levi's warm hand in mine. I don't want to talk anymore. Pouring all of this out has made me tired, to the point that I don't want to write in my journal either.

The hinges of the door squeak, and Yvonne comes into the room. "I need to go home for a while. Do you want a lift, Katie?"

I sit up straight and angle my body towards her. "That would be lovely, thank you."

Yvonne and I walk out to the car park in silence. I'm nervous because I think the drive home is going to be uncomfortable, but when Yvonne smiles at me, I relax.

"He was excited about you coming home," she says once we're on the motorway. "He couldn't wait to see you."

"I'm sorry, about coming over … I didn't know how serious it was …"

"It's okay," Yvonne says. "We just have to pick ourselves up and deal with what life throws at us."

I bite my bottom lip. "Sometimes what it throws us totally sucks."

Yvonne chuckles. "Yes, it does. But on the up side, Levi opened his eyes the other day."

"He did?" I stare at her, wide eyed. "Did he say anything? Did you talk to him?"

Yvonne shakes her head. "The pain medication is keeping him pretty heavily sedated. He fell asleep again quite quickly, but it was nice to see his eyes." She smiles.

I would love to be able to look into Levi's eyes again.

We spend the rest of the trip in silence, and I listen to the noises rushing past us. I miss Levi already, and I wish I had a way to be close to him when I'm not at the hospital. The bougainvillea reminds me so much of Levi, but I can't sit on the trellis.

As we turn onto the highway, I think about all the places where I've been happy with Levi. The park when we had a picnic dinner. The small clearing at school. My bedroom. And the treehouse.

Yvonne pulls into her driveway and turns the car off. "How are you holding up, Katie?"

"Me?" I turn to her, ripped from my thoughts. "I always make it through."

"If you ever want to talk, just come and knock, okay?"

I nod, and we both get out of the car, moving towards our own houses.

"Yvonne?" I spin to face her again. "Can I ... go and sit in the treehouse?"

She smiles. "Of course. Any time you like."

I wait until she's inside, then I make my way down the side of Levi's house to the backyard. It feels like an eternity since I've set foot down here, and so many memories come flooding back. It's as if I can see Mason and Levi, and Daniel and me, all chasing each other, our laughter filling the air.

In the back corner of the yard sits the treehouse, built into the branches of a gum tree. As I make my way towards it, I remember the day the four of us started building it. Mason and Daniel thought they knew what they were doing, but after Mason hit himself on the thumb with a hammer, his dad ended up finishing the platform for us. That's how I remember Levi's dad. He always helped if we asked, but I don't remember him smiling much.

I stop at the base of the tree and put my foot on the bottom step. We made them from timber offcuts and nailed them to the trunk. I climb up and crawl onto the floor of the treehouse. It has a roof made from tin sheets, but only two walls, one along the back and one along one side. The back wall has a square cut out of it, and the purple curtains I made so long ago are still here, although they're worn and faded now. I touch them with my fingertips and smile.

In the corner is an old wooden kids table-and-chair set. The seats seem so small now, but I pull one out and sit on it, setting my journal and purse on the scratched table. For a moment I sit and take it all in. The four of us spent so much time up here when we were kids. It feels like home.

I adjust myself in the seat, and my foot bumps something under the table. There's a shoebox shoved into the back corner, and I reach in to pull it out. I've never seen it before. We never had much stuff up here because the four of us took up all the space. I set the box on the table and stare at the lid. It's not very dusty, so it can't have been up here long. Either that, or it gets used a lot.

Maybe I shouldn't open it. It's not mine.

I put my fingers under the lip of the lid and take it off.

The box is filled with envelopes neatly stacked from front to back like a filing cabinet, and the one at the front has my name written on it. I flip it forward, and the next one has my name on it as well. When I riffle through the rest of them, they're all addressed to me, and each one has a date on the back.

I'm pretty sure it's Levi's handwriting.

Has he written me a box of letters?

Why didn't he give them to me?

Am I supposed to read them? Maybe not, if he never actually gave them to me. I look around at the treehouse with its two walls and dirty curtains. How often does he come up here? I take out the first letter. The date on the back is the day Josephine died, which means Levi must have written it before the accident. I take out the last letter, and the date on the back of that one is the day of Mason's death.

Has he been writing to me this whole time? Why would he do that? For so many years I thought he didn't want to have anything to do with me because he wouldn't talk to me, and Levi was writing to me instead.

My eyes blur, and a tear drips from my cheek onto the envelope in my hand.

How can I possibly read these? What if I don't want to know what's in them?

The past should stay where it is. We're supposed to be looking to our future.

"Knock, knock."

I look up as Daniel's head pops over the floor of the treehouse. He climbs the rest of the way and sits on the edge of the platform. I swipe at the tears rolling down my cheeks.

"You didn't need a lift?" Daniel asks.

I'm glad he didn't ask if I'm okay. "Yvonne drove me home."

"I know, I was just talking to her. She said you were up here. What's that?" Daniel points to the box.

"A shoebox."

Daniel laughs. "Really, Katie? What's *in* it?"

I stare down at the envelopes all lined up neatly. "They must be letters, but I haven't opened any yet."

"Who are they addressed to?"

"Me," I say. "I think Levi has been writing to me."

"If they have your name on them, read them."

"There must be a reason why he never gave them to me," I say. "He might not want me to know what's written in them. Like I don't want anyone to read my journal. Reading these without his permission would be invading his privacy."

Daniel shrugs. "Do what you think is right."

I take a deep breath then place the lid back on and crouch down to put the box back where I found it. "Maybe I'll ask him about them when he's awake."

"Come on," Daniel says. "Dinner's ready."

I follow my brother down the rungs of the treehouse and through Levi's backyard. The night is clear, and as I cross the boundary into our front yard, a star blazes in the blackness. I say a prayer for Levi, and then I wish for everything to work out, hoping it will come true.

5

What is the point?

Levi has been off the respirator for a while now, but he hasn't been awake any of the times I've been to see him. His waking moments are few due to the sedation, but I wish he would wake up long enough to know I'm here. It's hard not knowing if he can hear me.

Since finding the letters, I haven't talked about them to Levi, and it's eating away at me. Why did he write them? What did he write in them?

I sit in the chair beside his bed and pull my journal out, tapping my pen against the cover while I stare at the tinsel and Christmas baubles the nurses have put up around the room.

I've managed to form a routine with my visits. I come about an hour after visiting time starts, so Yvonne can be here for a while first, then when I arrive she gives me some time to spend with Levi alone. I always start with writing in my journal, then I sit and talk to him.

The paper rustles as I open the small book to a fresh page. I'm finally able to use the one Karen gave me for my birthday because my other one is full, and remembering the day she gave it to me makes me smile. It seems so long ago.

"I'm going to write for a bit," I say to Levi. "Don't go anywhere, okay?"

I press my pen to the page ...

Levi hasn't been awake during my visits. They say he's too heavily sedated to have many periods of consciousness. Yvonne assures me he has been awake, although never for very long, and even she isn't sure if he knows what's going on yet. Apparently he needs to be sedated in order for his body to rest and heal.

I want him to wake up.

I want to tell him I love him, and that I'm so sorry for not trying harder.

I haven't told him I found the letters yet. I'm not sure if I should mention them at all. Maybe they were hidden because he doesn't want me to read them. But why would he have kept them?

I have so many questions for him.

Please, wake up, Levi.

I need you.

Levi groans softly, and I look up from my page. His head moves, and I stand, my journal and pen dropping to the floor. The pen rolls under the bed.

"Levi?" I ask.

He doesn't respond.

I take his hand, and he moves his head again, but he doesn't open his eyes. His lips part and I hold my breath, waiting to see if he'll say something. I squeeze his hand and his fingers move, curling around mine.

"Levi," I say again. "Are you awake?"

He groans again, and his head settles back to the side. His eyes stay closed. I sit back in the chair, still holding his hand. The door opens and the nurse comes in.

"How are you, Katie?" she asks, coming to the foot of the bed and looking at Levi's chart.

"I'm good … I think Levi is waking up."

The nurse looks up and goes around to the other side of the bed. "We've been lowering his dosage slightly each day, so any time from now he can become fully aware. Just keep talking to him." She smiles. "Everything looks good though. His vitals are fine, and his readings are where they should be."

"Thank you," I say.

The nurse leaves, and I turn back to Levi. A tear rolls down my cheek, and I swat it away with my free hand.

"Look at me crying again. You'd think I'd done enough of that." I stare at him, hoping for a response. When I don't get one I continue, "You remember when I told you we had Josie's funeral? I came to see you after, and your mum drove me home." I pause. "I wanted to be close to you, so I went to sit in the treehouse. It hasn't changed much. Although the curtains could do with a wash." I smile. "I sat up there for a while, thinking about a lot of stuff. How happy we were when we were kids. The fun we used to have. I miss that. I miss what we used to have before … anyway. I found something while I was up there." I stop again, and trace circles on the back of Levi's hand with my thumb. "I found a shoebox filled with envelopes with my name on them. And I so desperately want you to wake up, because I want to talk to you about them."

More tears spill onto my cheeks, and I rest my forehead against the bedrail.

"I haven't read any of them yet. Daniel said I should if they're addressed to me. But what if you don't want me to read them?" I look at him again, my eyes hot. "And they're all about the past, right? Do I want to revisit that? Do I want to know what you wrote back then but couldn't for whatever reason tell me? Because the past is in the past, isn't it? And how can we move forward if we keep dwelling on it?"

I try to hold the tears in, but more come and I can't stop them, and within seconds I'm sobbing, my shoulders shaking. *Wake up! Please.*

My vision blurs, and I glance up at the decorations on the walls, the red and gold baubles blobs of colour against the stark hospital walls. Christmas will be here soon. I want to spend it with Levi. How can I spend it without him? How will I get through another day without him?

"It's not fair," I whisper in between gulps of air.

A hand touches my shoulder and I sit back, surprised to see Yvonne. I hadn't even heard her come in.

"The doctors say he'll make a full recovery," she says.

I sniffle and let go of Levi's hand so I can stand. "I know. I just …"

She offers me a small smile. "I know. Me, too."

Yvonne wraps me up in her arms, hugging me like every mother knows how to hug her child. Even though she's not my mum, I'm so grateful to have her here.

I pull away. "Thank you. But I'm the one who should be comforting you."

She tucks my hair behind my ear. "Maybe we can comfort each other. I'm very happy that you're here for Levi."

We sit together for a while, but as the seconds tick by, I don't have anything I want to say to Yvonne, and I don't feel comfortable talking to Levi in front of her.

"I should go," I say, getting to my feet.

Yvonne nods. I gather my things and head towards the door, glancing back at Levi and his mum. She has already taken the seat beside the bed and is holding his hand. I slip quietly out the door and take a deep breath to pull myself together.

On my way through the ICU I pull my phone out to text Daniel. He said he'd come and get me when I was ready. He'd just be hanging around over at the shopping centre. I wait until I'm out of the ward and in the main part of the hospital before I pull up his number and send him a quick message.

Veronica, Jarred, and Geoff come into the hospital foyer. Veronica smiles, and the three of them walk over to me.

"You've been crying?" Veronica frowns.

I push my glasses up my nose and look at my phone. "Um ... yeah."

She doesn't ask me why or if I'm okay, and I let out a breath.

"How is he?" Jarred asks.

"You haven't seen him yet?" I put my phone away and look at him.

Jarred shakes his head, and I sense that he's mad, but I'm not sure if it's directed at me or at the fact he hasn't been able to see his best friend.

His friend who was driving the car that killed his girlfriend.

I blink a few times to settle the heat pricking at my eyes.

"They told us family only," Geoff says. "You're not family."

I bite my lip. "I thought you guys would have been able to see him by now."

"You didn't answer my question," Jarred says.

I fiddle with the ends of my hair. "He's ... they say he'll be fine. But it's going to take a while."

The four of us stand there, staring at each other. I don't know what else to tell them. It's hard to explain what Levi looks like. And when I think about him, I want to cry again.

"You should ask Yvonne if you can see him," I say. "They only let two visitors at a time into his room though."

"Is she here?" Veronica asks.

"Yeah." I glance at the reception desk then lower my voice. "Use the phone on the wall at the entrance to the ICU, and ask for her. Hopefully she'll say you can see him."

Geoff walks off without saying anything else. I probably shouldn't expect a thank you from him, but I thought we'd made some progress while we were at Surfers Paradise. His arrogance now makes me dislike him all over again.

"Thanks, Katie," Jarred says, following his friend.

I offer him a small smile, and hope he does get to see Levi. If I hadn't been able to all this time I think I'd be crazy by now.

Veronica hangs back. She purses her lips and adjusts the strap of her bag on her shoulder. Her mouth opens, then she closes it again.

"What's wrong?" I ask. "Is there something you want to say?"

She takes a breath. "I just … I'm having a New Year's party, and I thought maybe you'd like to come? If you're around, that is."

I chew the side of my thumb. "I don't have a very good track record with your parties."

We stare at each other for a second, then both laugh. I'm surprised at how good it feels. I haven't laughed in what seems like ages.

"Dad's booked me a couple of hotel rooms overlooking the harbour." Veronica shifts on her feet. "He said I can ask my friends if I like."

Does she think of me as a friend now?

"Harbour views, on New Year's?" I don't hide my shock very well. "That sounds … expensive."

I drop my gaze because despite the fact we're no longer in school, Veronica and I are very different people. Something she used to like reminding me of on a regular basis.

"Come on, Katie. It'll be fun."

I look up. "Why do you even want me there?"

Veronica folds her arms and squares her shoulders. "You don't *have* to come. I just thought … you know …" She looks away, then at the floor, then back at me. "New year, new opportunities. A fresh start?"

I'm quiet for a few heartbeats, trying to figure out if she's somehow asking me to be friends with her.

"A party sounds great," I eventually say. "We could all use some cheering up."

"Hey, Ronnie," Jarred calls along the hallway. He's standing at the turn that leads to the ICU. "You coming?"

She waves at him then turns back to me. "I better go." She takes a few steps. "Bring Karen. I've already asked Jess and Stacey."

I nod, and watch her walk towards Jarred, before going outside into the warm summer air. Daniel is waiting for me on the street. He smiles as I slide into the passenger seat.

"How is he today?" he asks.

"No change really," I say. "He did groan. The nurse says he has some moments when he's awake and more aware, but they're not often. They're weaning him off the sedatives, so hopefully he'll wake up soon." I look at my brother, fresh tears in my eyes. "I want to hear his voice."

Daniel reaches over and squeezes my hand before pulling the car out onto the street. We head for the motorway, and I wind the window down a bit to get some fresh air on my face. I settle my head back against the headrest.

"You should go see Jess when we get home," Daniel says. "She's not doing so well today."

I roll my head to the side to look at Daniel, studying him for a moment. "You went to see her this morning?"

He nods. "I'm not sure how to help her though."

"Yeah, it's hard." I chew my lip and glance sideways at my brother. "You're really worried, aren't you?"

"Well, yeah." He shrugs. "It's Jess."

"Is there something you're not telling me?"

Daniel glances at me sideways. "Like what?"

I sit up straight in my seat. "Like you … and Jess—"

"Can't I be worried?"

I smile and decide not to push him. "Of course you can. I'll go and see her."

We don't talk for the rest of the trip. Daniel parks the car in our driveway and we get out. He glances at me and smiles, but his eyes don't have their usual sparkle. He makes his way towards the front door. His slumped shoulders tell me he's got something on his mind.

I watch him for a second before calling out, "Hey. Want to come with me?" Daniel turns when he reaches the door. "I'm sure Jess would love to see you again, too."

Daniel comes back to where I'm standing on the grass. "I'd like that."

He doesn't say anything else, and we walk together down the street to Jessica's place. Her mum lets us in. She seems a little better today.

"Jess is in her room," Bridget says.

"How is she?" I ask.

Jessica's mum purses her lips and takes a deep breath. "She's … not coping very well. She won't look in the mirror, and I can't get her out of her room. Maybe …" She stares at me and a tear rolls down her cheek. I hug her because I'm not sure what else to do, and sometimes a hug makes you feel better when words can't.

"We'll just sit with her for a bit," Daniel says.

I pull away from Bridget, and Daniel puts a hand on my shoulder. We go downstairs to Jessica's bedroom where we find her sitting in her desk chair, staring out the window. She doesn't look at us when we come into the room.

Jessica is still in her pyjamas, the bed is unmade, and there's a towel taped to the wardrobe door, covering the mirror. Daniel and I exchange a glance.

I sit on the edge of the bed and face Jessica. "Hey. We thought you might like some company."

Daniel sits beside me. "Maybe we could go for a walk?"

Jessica finally looks at us. "I don't feel up to a walk."

I look out the window at the bush that backs onto the houses on our side of the street. Jessica's house is farther back on the block than Levi's and mine, so there isn't much backyard, but the view down into the valley is pretty.

"We could go upstairs and sit on the balcony," I say. "Look at the trees and listen to the birds."

Jessica smiles with her lips closed. "Can we just sit here?"

"Sure," I say.

Daniel shuffles back on the bed so he's leaning against the wall under the window. I'm not exactly sure what to do, so I stand and tidy the room a bit, arranging the things on Jessica's side table, putting rubbish in her bin, and taking the dirty clothes to the laundry.

When I get back I stop in the doorway, then quickly step into the hall again. Jessica has moved to the bed to sit with Daniel. He has his arm around her, and I have to stop myself from frowning. I peek around the doorjamb at them.

Jessica looks up at my brother and smiles. A weight lifts from my shoulders, because I haven't seen her smile in what feels like forever. Daniel leans down and kisses her softly on the lips, and I step back again. I shouldn't be watching this. It's their private moment, but I peek around the door jamb again because it's so nice to see Jessica happy.

"Katie?" Karen whispers in my ear, and I jump. "What are you doing?"

"Oh my God, you scared me," I whisper back.

Stacey comes down the stairs.

"Thought I should be quiet." Karen keeps her voice low. "Since you're already spying on Jess."

"Why are we whispering?" Stacey looks from Karen to me. "What's going on?"

I point to Jessica's room. "Daniel and Jess … he kissed her."

"What?" Karen says, then claps a hand over her mouth.

I cringe. "Maybe we should leave."

"You don't have to go," Daniel calls. "You think we can't hear you?"

I step into the doorway. "I know you heard Karen."

She laughs, and pushes me into the room. Stacey follows.

"Hi girls," Daniel says.

I sit in the desk chair and glance sideways at my brother. Karen dumps a shopping bag on the floor, and Stacey puts another one beside it.

"I'm glad we're all here," Karen says. "Stacey and I brought supplies."

"We've got chocolate, and lollies, and chips, and tea, and DVDs." Stacey kneels on the floor and unpacks one of the bags.

"All the stuff we need for an afternoon in." Karen plonks down beside Stacey.

I smile at my friends, and wish I had been a part of organising this for Jessica. Instead, I've been wrapped up in going to see Levi. I really want to talk to my friends about him, but I'm scared Jessica won't want to hear his name. I'm not sure how she feels about Levi at the moment. Even if Josephine ran that stop sign, he was still driving the car that killed her.

"I should probably go," Daniel says. "You girls look like you have a busy afternoon ahead of you."

Jessica bites her lip and looks at him. She doesn't say anything, but from the way she's gripping his hand, I don't think she wants him to leave.

"Don't be stupid," Karen says, glancing from Jessica to me. "You can stay."

Karen rips open a family-sized block of chocolate, passing it to me. I break off a few pieces then toss it onto the bed for Jessica and Daniel. For the next half an hour we stuff our faces, and talk about Christmas.

"Anyone going away?" Karen asks.

"Nope, we'll be at home," I say, smiling at Daniel.

Jessica shakes her head. "Staying home, too. Mum cancelled everything."

"We have to go up the coast to Nan's place," Stacey says, crinkling her nose. "It's always noisy."

"Well, I'm being dragged down south to my aunt's," Karen says. "Four nights of sleeping on the floor in my cousin's room."

"You love it," I say, smiling.

"Yeah, the little rug rats are kinda cute."

"What's everyone getting for Christmas?" Stacey asks.

"I want my own car," Karen says, popping a piece of

chocolate in her mouth. "But that's never going to happen. I usually ask for money so I can go shopping at the sales in the new year."

"Socks," Daniel says, smiling. "I need socks."

We all laugh.

"The presents don't matter so much," I say. "I just like being with fam …" I stop before I finish the word, but it's too late.

The room goes quiet.

The smile drops from Jessica's face. She snuggles down into the crook of Daniel's arm, looks at her hands, and takes a deep breath. I'm such an idiot for talking about family. Jessica is missing a piece of hers.

"I'm sorry … Jess, I … I'm sorry," I stutter.

"It's okay." She sniffles, and tucks her hair behind her ear. "Family is really important. And friends are, too." She looks up and stares at me. "How's Levi?"

I open my mouth to reply, but no sound comes out. How do I answer that question? He's lying broken in a hospital bed.

"He's … they say he'll be fine." I drop my gaze and pull my knees to my chest, resting my heels on the edge of the chair. "He's not awake properly yet, so I haven't … he hasn't talked to anyone."

The room falls quiet again.

A kookaburra laughs outside.

We all avoid looking at each other.

"Oh!" Karen says, breaking the silence. "I got two acceptance letters yesterday."

"That's great," Daniel says. "Where to?"

"One for Newcastle, and one for Macquarie."

"I got a letter from Sydney Uni," Stacey says.

"Let me guess." I rest my chin on my knees. "Vet science?"

"Yep." She grins.

"What course were you accepted into, Karen?" I ask.

"Psychology." She opens a packet of chips and stuffs some in her mouth before passing them to Stacey. "Think I'll go to Newcastle."

"I got into Newcastle as well," Jessica says, quietly. "For their communications degree. I think I'd like a career in journalism … someday."

"What do you mean, someday?" I ask.

Jessica looks at me with sad eyes. "I've always wanted a year off to travel. Josie was going to come with me. Now, I don't know what I want to do. With Josie gone …" She shrugs, and stares down at the bed. "What's the point? Why go to uni, or travel, or do anything, when I could die tomorrow? Any of us could …"

Jessica's voice trails off, and the air in the room becomes heavy with sadness.

"Have you opened your letters yet?" Karen breaks the silence and raises her eyebrows at me.

"No, she hasn't." Daniel frowns, taking the chips from Stacey and shoving some in his mouth.

Jessica is still staring at the bed, worrying at the side of her thumb.

My future isn't something I want to think about right now.

I stare at my brother and shrug. "Maybe Jess has the right idea. What *is* the point?"

6

So hard

I open my eyes on Christmas morning and stare at the stars on my ceiling, wondering how I'm going to get through the day. I guess I just have to focus on what I have rather than what I don't. Try and be grateful that my brother is alive, my parents aren't fighting, and that I have a wonderful family who loves me.

But it's going to be hard, because even though I have so much to be thankful for, I still have holes in my heart that need fixing.

I've been visiting Levi as much as I can during the past week. On a couple of occasions I couldn't go in to see him, because the doctors were in with him doing tests or physio or other doctor stuff, and the times I did get to sit with him, he still wasn't conscious enough to talk to me. He's moving his head around a bit though, so hopefully next time I see him he'll be awake.

I can't wait to hear his voice.

I managed to get some last-minute Christmas shopping done, and I've seen Jessica every other day as well. She's been spending more time with Daniel, which is a good thing, but I'm worried about her. She seems to have lost all motivation for anything. I can relate to how she feels, and I want to help her, but I'm not sure how. Today will be a sad day for her and her parents without having Josephine.

"Merry Christmas," Daniel says from the other side of my door.

I stretch and roll onto my side. "You can come in."

The door opens and my brother sticks his head around it, smiling. "Get up. There're presents under the tree."

I fake a yawn. "I want to stay here."

Daniel pushes the door open all the way. "Come on, Katie." His smile widens, and he pulls a Santa hat onto his head.

I laugh and throw my covers back, getting out of bed. "You're such a dork."

I quickly wash my face and follow my brother downstairs. Mum is in the kitchen with the oven already on. It's going to get a workout today. Shortbread cookies are the first thing on the menu, by the looks of it.

"Merry Christmas, you two," Mum says, wrapping both of us in a hug.

"Where's Dad?" I ask.

"He's gone to the bakery to get the bread rolls."

"You mean we have to wait to open presents?" Daniel asks.

"No more waiting." Dad comes into the kitchen and puts a bag full of rolls on the bench. "Let's go. Presents." He rubs his hands together.

We all pile into the lounge room and sit on the floor around the Christmas tree. I'm not excited because I want to find out what I got. I'm excited because I want to see everyone else's faces when they open their presents. We've never done big expensive gifts because we've never been able to, but I always love seeing how happy even the smallest gift can make someone.

"Who wants to be Santa?" Dad asks.

"Daniel's wearing the hat," I say.

"All right then." Daniel jumps up and goes to sit beside the tree.

He hands out the presents until the base of the tree is bare. Then we all start ripping paper. Mum smiles at the pair of silver earrings I bought her, putting them in straight away. I got Dad a book, and he starts reading it as soon as he opens it. Daniel laughs at his metal Slinky, and I grin.

"Open your presents, Katie," Daniel says.

I rip open the parcel from my brother. It's a beautiful pen and a new set of headphones. I pick up my present from Mum and Dad, smiling because I think it's another notebook or journal. It's definitely shaped like one, although it must be in a box. Maybe it's a writing set.

"Have you looked at your results yet?" Mum asks.

I slip my finger under the edge of the wrapping paper. "No, and I told you, I don't want to."

"Well, we think you should," Dad says.

I look up at him and frown. "You looked?"

"We're so proud of you, honey." Mum's grin is so wide she's going to split her cheeks.

"You looked?" I ask again. "When you knew I didn't want to?"

"Katie," Dad says. "You got in the top two percent of the state."

"Open your present," Mum says. "We got you something special for doing so well."

I should be happy that I got such good marks, but does any of it even matter? I look down at the package in my hands, my finger still under the edge of the wrapping paper. What have they bought me? It does feel heavier than a normal notebook. I frown and rip the paper back, letting it fall to the floor.

I stare at the box with a picture of a small laptop on it.

"That's a pretty awesome present," Daniel says.

My mouth drops open. I'm not sure what to say. I've never had my own computer. I'm lucky I have a phone.

"We thought you could use it for uni," Mum says. "You'll need something to do your assignments on."

"Thank you." I don't say anything else, because I don't want to sound ungrateful, but how can they afford this? We already have a computer; I can use that. I turn the box over to look at the details and a folded piece of paper falls into my lap. I pick it up. "What's this?"

"You got into Newcastle and Macquarie Universities." Mum's grin widens.

I stare at the letters. "You opened my mail as well?"

"Honey, you need to make your decision before it's too late."

I set the computer box on the floor and the letters on

top of it, then stand. "You had no right to open my mail."

Dad gets to his feet. "Now, hang on a minute. We've given you space after what happened with Levi and Josephine, but you need to step up, Katherine. We have every right to make sure your future is secure."

"By expecting me to do something I don't want to?" I yell.

"What do you mean?" Mum asks as she gets to her feet as well.

"Law or medicine, Mum." Tears prick my eyes and heat seeps into my cheeks. "I've never been allowed another choice."

"But … that's what you always wanted to do." Mum frowns.

"No." I shake my head. "It's what *you* want me to do."

"If not a lawyer or a doctor, then what?" Dad asks.

Air puffs out of my mouth in short breaths. "You have no idea, do you? You've never actually asked me what I want to do with my life, until now."

"Katie, calm down," Daniel says from his seat on the floor.

"I don't want to be calm," I shout. "All my life I've tried to be better than I really am. I've tried to fit in with what everyone else wants, and be who everyone wants me to be. I'm smart, so I must want to use my brains for a high-profile, highly academic career. What about what *I* want?"

"Tell us, Katie," Dad says. "Tell us what you want."

"Right now, I want Levi to get better." Tears stream down my cheeks, and I clench my fingers. "I want him to wake up, and I want to hear his voice. Until then, I can't think about the future."

Mum takes a step towards me, her face twisted into a teary grimace. "Katie ..."

I turn away from her and run to the front door, yanking it open. I don't stop to put my shoes on, racing across the grass and through the garden bed to Levi's yard. I hurry down the side of his house, the rough ground cutting into my bare feet, but I don't care. I keep going, my vision blurry from my tears, until I reach the treehouse.

At the top of the steps I haul myself onto the platform and crawl to the little table in the corner. I swipe at my eyes to clear them, then pull a chair out and sit. My lungs heave as I take deep breaths to try and calm myself, but I can't. It's all too much.

I look out at the morning sunlight through the branches of the tree. A light breeze tousles the leaves, and shadows dance on the ground below. I stare at the way they move sporadically, and I feel that chaos in the pit of my stomach.

A sob rises into my chest, and I squeeze my eyes closed. I try not to let it free, but I can't help it. My mouth opens, and out comes a sound so heartbreaking it makes me cry harder. My shoulders shake, and I grip the edge of the table. I shove it, releasing a burst of anger, and it bangs against the wall. I pound my fist on the tabletop, and the impact vibrates up my arm. I hit it again, with both fists this time, again, and again, and again, until my hands ache. But still, it's not enough.

The pain is not enough.

I need something else to hurt just as much as my heart.

I kneel on the floor and grab the chair, swinging it so it hits one of the walls. It makes a loud crash, but it doesn't break. I swing again, and again, and the chair cracks. One more swing and a leg catches on the curtains, ripping them down. I crawl along the floor, looping my fingers into any hole I can find in the fabric, and tearing until the curtains are shredded.

Blood drips onto the floor from a cut on my index finger. I sit on the wood, rest my hands in my lap, and stare at them, my shoulders heaving from the effort and the tears. Why is everything so hard? In frustration, I kick out with my legs and knock the table. It topples onto its side.

My breath catches in my throat at the sight of the shoebox in the corner.

Levi's letters.

I stare at the box for a while, waiting for my heartbeat to slow, and my breathing to even out. After a couple of minutes, I wipe my hands on what's left of the curtains. The cut on my finger stings, and I suck on it. The coppery taste of my blood fills my mouth.

"Katie?" Daniel says, and I look over the edge of the platform.

"I don't want to talk right now," I say.

He stares up at me. "I just want to make sure—"

"That I'm okay?" I snort. "No. I'm not."

"Please come back inside." Daniel glances towards our house. "Mum's taken the cookies out of the oven."

I move away from the edge so I don't have to look at my brother. "Maybe later. Please go away."

Daniel doesn't reply. I listen for a few heartbeats then I crawl to the corner and retrieve the shoebox, sitting with my back against the wall with the box in my lap.

"What happened in here?" Daniel comes into the treehouse and sits with his legs hanging over the edge.

"I did a little remodelling," I say.

Daniel smiles but it doesn't reach his eyes, and his sadness radiates from him like the pain must be radiating from me. I rest my hands on top of the shoebox and study my brother. Sisterly intuition tells me he's worried about something other than me.

"You read any of those yet?" He points to the box.

I shake my head. "Daniel … are you … is there something you want to talk about?"

"Are you changing the subject?"

"No." I cross my legs under me and set the box to the side. "I can tell when something's bothering you."

"I'm worried about you, Katie."

I shake my head again. "It's not that. Tell me. You already know everything that's bothering me."

Daniel chuckles. "Yeah."

We stare at each other for a moment.

"Seriously," I say. "You can talk to me."

Daniel takes a deep breath, and adjusts his position on the edge of the platform. "It's Jess. She's … in a really bad place."

"Her sister died," I say. "I think she's allowed to be."

"She won't look in the mirror. She says every time she does, all she sees is Josie. And she's been having, like mini breakdowns. Bursts of violence." Daniel runs a hand down his face.

I look around the treehouse. "I can relate to that."

"This is different. She … she smashed a mirror the other day and cut her hands."

"Oh ... I hadn't noticed."

We both go silent.

I've been too caught up in myself and Levi.

I'm a terrible friend.

"Does she talk to you?" Daniel asks. "About Josie? About anything?"

I pull my knees up to my chest and hug my legs. "No. We mostly hang out and listen to music. She's like she was last week when we were all there. She talks, but she hasn't told me anything about ... that night. Or about how she's feeling."

"Jess blames herself." Daniel stares at his hands and picks at his fingernails. "She said she and Josie had a big fight over something. Josie wouldn't have gone out otherwise."

"Jess wasn't driving," I say. "She can't blame herself. She can't control other people's actions."

Daniel shrugs. "I've tried to tell her that." He looks up at me and his eyes are red. "I don't know how to help her."

"You really care about Jess?" I press my lips together. "When did this happen? How did I miss it?"

"You've been pretty caught up in your own stuff."

I glance down at the shoebox. "I guess I have."

"Are you coming home now? It's Christmas, and I want to spend it with my sister."

I tuck my hair behind my ear. "Give me fifteen minutes. I need to clean up in here."

Daniel nods and shuffles down onto the treehouse steps. "See you in a bit."

I watch my brother walk across Levi's backyard, then I set to work putting everything back. The chair will need some glue, but I'll worry about that later. I push the table into the corner, tuck the chairs under it, and rehang the curtains. They look worse than they did before. Now they have big tears in them, and some blood stains courtesy of the cut on my finger. The last item to put back is the shoebox.

I stare at the box on the floor of the treehouse. It needs to go under the table again, but I can't help opening it to take another look inside. I pull out the letter at the back of the box. The one with the oldest date on it. The date of Mason's death. I want to read it. It is addressed to me, so I should be allowed to, but will Levi be upset?

Would I be upset if he found and read a box of letters I'd written to him?

Maybe.

What if Levi read my journal? Would I be angry?

I run my finger over my name on the front of the envelope. I'm pretty sure I'd be devastated if Levi read my journal without asking, but even if he did read it, I don't have any dark secrets. I just write to make sense of my life and what's happened to me over the years. Maybe Levi wrote to me to try and do the same.

The envelope isn't sealed. I open the flap and carefully pull out the piece of paper that's inside. Then I settle back against the wall to read.

Dear Katie,

Mason died today.

That's probably not the best way to start a letter, but it's the truth. I've learnt the hard way that the truth really hurts.

Some other things that are true: I regret ignoring you.

I regret thinking I'm better than you. I want to climb in your window. I so badly want to talk to you. I need you. I miss you.

I know it's my fault that we're not friends anymore, and I wish I could change that, but I don't know how. You have every right to never speak to me again. And I haven't tried to fix things because I'm so scared you'll tell me no. That you'll tell me you don't want me in your life. It kills me to see you every day and not be able to talk to you like I used to.

I have so much to tell you.

Like how Mum and Dad fight all the time. And how it's my fault Mason is dead. Dad can't even look me in the eye. He's angry. I don't like being in the house, but now it's worse. I'm worried about Mum.

I so badly want to talk to you. I have no one to tell my secrets to.

I miss the way you used to listen.

I miss how you always knew what to say.

I miss your laugh.

I miss your smile.

I miss everything about you.

When I saw you after Mum told you all that he'd died, I wanted to tell you how beautiful you looked. I wanted to tell you that the look in your eyes at knowing my brother is dead explained exactly what I'm feeling. Because I know you must be hurting as well. I know you love my brother, too, and that losing him hurts more than words can describe.

I wanted to hold you, and cry in your arms, and mourn my brother with you. I wanted to tell you that life is too short to let go of the people we love.

Because I love you.

I love you, Katherine Sullivan.

And I will probably never get to tell you that.

I hope one day I can, because walking away from you is the biggest regret of my life.

I want to tell you everything, but now I'm afraid you won't listen, or you won't know what to say.

Levi.

A tear runs down my cheek and splashes onto the paper, marking it and making the ink run. The L in Levi's name blurs. I quickly fold the letter back in half and slip it into the envelope. Why didn't Levi give me this letter? Why didn't he talk to me? I would have listened to him. If only he had told me what he was going through, maybe finding my way back to Levi wouldn't have been so hard.

7

That stupid game

The rest of Christmas Day passed in a blur. Mum and Dad stepped around me, pretending nothing had happened, and we had our traditional family meal with ham, prawns, and pavlova for dessert. I fell into bed, exhausted physically and emotionally, and I didn't sleep well thinking about Levi's letters. I didn't read any more. I really want to ask him about them first.

Now it's New Year's Eve, and I'm sitting in the hard plastic chair beside Levi's bed, waiting for him to wake up enough to talk to me. He's improved over the past few days, having more periods of semi-consciousness. They're mostly in the mornings before visiting hours start, so by the time I get here he's already had his medication. He's opened his eyes a couple of times, but never long enough to focus on me.

Karen is back from her aunt's place, and we're going into the city for Veronica's party tonight, but I couldn't go without seeing Levi first. The nurses joke that I've become a permanent fixture in his room, and soon they'll have to start dusting me.

"I have to go soon," I say to Levi, squeezing his hand. "We're going into the city for New Year's. I wish you could come." I go quiet, waiting for a response, but as usual, there isn't one.

I've already told Levi about Christmas, and what happened with Mum and Dad, but I left out the part where I read one of his letters. I feel guilty, as if I've invaded his private thoughts. Which I have.

"I don't think I told you the other day that I went to the treehouse again. On Christmas morning." I chew my lip. "I was so upset at Mum and Dad, and I wanted to be close to you. I didn't know where else to go." Levi's eyelids flutter, and I lean forward. "Can you hear me, Levi?"

I wait again, but he's still.

"I had a ... an outburst. One of the chairs will need fixing, and there're some holes in the curtains ... Anyway, I ... I read one of your letters." I stop again and press my forehead to the bedrail. The metal is cool against my skin. "Please don't be angry with me. But I want you to know, from now on, I will always listen."

A tear rolls down my cheek and splashes onto the bed sheet. I stare at the small wet mark, and take a deep breath before sitting up straight in the chair.

"I have to go, okay? I'll come and see you tomorrow. Next year." I smile and squeeze his hand, then get to my feet.

The door opens and Karen sticks her head in. "You

ready?"

"Ready." I nod, then follow my best friend out of the hospital and to the car.

We haven't had a chance to talk much with her being away, so I haven't told Karen about what happened. I don't get the chance though, because Karen's mouth is going a million miles an hour, telling me about her Christmas.

"Sounds like you had a great time," I say, smiling.

"Have you packed anything for tonight yet?" Karen asks as we merge onto the motorway.

I raise my eyebrows at her. "It's one night. I'm sure I can grab something when we get to my place."

She shakes her head. "What am I going to do with you?"

I chuckle and stare out the window for the rest of the ride home. When we reach my house, Karen and I grab a quick sandwich for lunch before heading to my room. We don't have to be on the train to the city until later, so I sit on the bed and watch Karen pack my carry-on suitcase with a heap of stuff I won't need.

"One night." I stare at Karen. "Which word do you not understand?"

"A girl needs to be prepared." She folds three tops and puts them in the case on top of my jeans.

"I'm sure I'll only need one change of clothes, my pyjamas, and my toothbrush."

Karen tsks at me. "Phone, purse, keys, contacts, makeup."

"All in my tote bag already."

Karen raises her eyebrows. "Lip gloss does not count as makeup."

"Fine, I'll get my powder, but that's it." I push off the bed and go to the door. "We're staying in a hotel overlooking the harbour. I don't think we'll be going anywhere."

"Get your eyeliner as well." Karen smiles.

I roll my eyes and go down the hall to the bathroom, grabbing my small makeup bag. I may as well take the whole thing. That way Karen will leave me alone.

Back in my room I change into my denim skirt and a clean singlet top, then we jump in the car to go to Karen's.

My phone buzzes with a message as she pulls into her driveway. Karen parks in front of the double garage, and we both get out of the car.

"I'll be five minutes," Karen says, popping the boot with the button on the car keys. "Then we can walk up to the train."

"Sure." I wave a hand at her and look at my phone. "Message from Mum."

I haven't spoken to Mum or Dad much since my fight with them on Christmas Day. I'm still upset that Mum opened my mail. I stare at her message.

Mum: Have a nice time 2night

Even though she said exactly the same thing to me this morning before I left the house, her message makes me smile.

Me: Okay

Mum: See you next year :)

I laugh out loud and smile wider, because I not too long ago said the same thing to Levi.

Me: Funny

Mum: Stay safe. Don't drink too much

Me: Stop worrying

Mum: It's my job

Mum: I love you

Me: I know. Luv U2

"Ready?" Karen asks.

"Hang on." I put my phone away and go around to the back of the car to grab my little case before closing the boot. "Let's go."

Karen and I walk the short distance to the train station, our suitcases bumping along the cracks in the footpath. We jump on the first train to the city, and settle into some seats upstairs for the forty-five-minute journey.

"How was your Christmas?" Karen asks.

I stare at her and bite my lip. "I had a fight with Mum and Dad and ran out of the house."

"Ouch. What was it about?"

I sigh. "Uni letters."

"You still haven't opened them?"

I tuck my hair behind my ear and look out the window. "Mum did it for me. I was so angry."

"So you read them? You need to decide which one you want to go to."

I look back at Karen and her raised eyebrows. "Yes, I eventually read them. I've been accepted into law at Newcastle and medicine at Macquarie. But you know I applied at the Sydney College of the Arts for a fine arts degree. They haven't sent me a letter yet."

"Well, maybe you can reapply to do fine arts at Newcastle, and we can go to uni together." Karen smiles.

"There's no way Mum will agree to let me do anything arts-based. She doesn't think my career opportunities will be good enough … I really want to go to SCA. I didn't tell Mum and Dad I applied." I shrug. "I don't want to do law or medicine and I figured if I got into SCA, I could convince them somehow. But I can't do that without an acceptance letter."

Karen folds her arms and huffs. "You shouldn't have to keep her happy."

"Tell her that. It doesn't matter anyway. If I was going to get in I would've gotten my letter by now."

Karen nudges my shoulder. "It'll work out."

I offer her a small smile, then look out the window for the rest of the trip. I hope everything does work out, but right now it doesn't seem promising. All I want to do is focus on having a good time on the last night of the year.

The train pulls into North Sydney Station and we get off, making our way out to the street. The hotel Veronica has booked is a five-minute walk, so we roll our cases down the hill until we reach the front driveway. I tell the receptionist we're with Veronica Porter and give her our names.

She smiles with her lips closed. "ID please." We both flash our drivers' licenses while she taps on her keyboard. She hands me a room key. "Floor eleven. Enjoy your stay."

"Thank you." I smile back then follow Karen to the lifts.

"She didn't look too impressed," Karen says as we get in.

I press number eleven. "Would you be if you had to work tonight?"

"I guess not."

We get out on the eleventh floor and follow the signs to the room. We stop outside and I glance at Karen.

"Let's get this party started." She smiles.

I have a room key, but I don't want to be rude, so I raise my hand and knock on the door. Shuffling and voices sound from inside. Then the door swings open.

"Hello!" Veronica cries. "Welcome to party central. Only fun allowed."

I chuckle and look Veronica up and down. Her cocktail dress and stilettoes make me feel inadequate in my denim skirt and singlet top. With a deep breath, I grin back at her and step into the hotel suite, holding the door for Karen. It clicks closed behind us and I glance around at the sitting room. There's a table set up with snacks and drinks, and streamers hang from the light fittings.

"Chuck your bags in the second bedroom," Veronica says, pointing to a door behind the small dining nook. "Then come join us on the balcony."

I crane my neck to have a look. Rachel is outside standing at the balcony railing, a glass of champagne in her hand. Stacey and Jessica are sitting at a small table and they jump up when they see us, coming inside. A door in the far corner stands slightly ajar.

"Hey." I smile at my friends.

"Yay, you're finally here," Stacey says.

I point to the internal door. "Is there a third bedroom?"

"We have adjoining suites," Veronica says. "Plenty of beds for everyone, although we have to fight over who gets to sleep with the boys."

Karen crosses her arm. "I don't think we'll be fighting."

"I don't think we'll be sleeping." Veronica laughs.

"Tonight is going to be so much fun," Stacey says, clapping her hands like a little kid.

Veronica grins. "That's the plan."

Stacey's smile is so wide it looks like her cheeks are hurting. Jessica is quiet beside her.

Karen and I put our stuff in the bedroom, then join the others on the balcony. Veronica hands us both a glass of champagne. I accept it, but make a mental note to sip it slowly. I don't want to end up drunk again. It wasn't much fun.

"Don't drink that too fast."

I glance over to the neighbouring balcony where Geoff is leaning against the railing, and Jarred is sitting at the small table. Both of them have beers in their hands.

"I'll make sure I don't," I say.

"Wouldn't want you throwing up on anyone," Geoff teases.

I frown. "How do you ... who told you I did that?" I don't remember anyone being there other than my friends and Levi.

"Word travels," Jarred says.

I glance around at my friends. I'm not angry that someone said something, I just don't want to remember that night. It wasn't a very good one.

"It's not like you've never been drunk and done something stupid before." Karen raises her eyebrows at Geoff.

He chuckles. "Fair enough."

"Can we just have a good time tonight?" Veronica says. "Tomorrow is a new year. We can put all the crap from this one behind us."

"I'll drink to that." Stacey raises her glass and takes a sip.

"We need music," Veronica says. She goes inside and comes back out with her phone and a small speaker.

"What should we listen to?"

"Anything," Rachel says, putting her feet up on the railing. "As long as it's loud."

She glances at me and scoffs before turning back to her drink and the view over the harbour. I know Rachel doesn't like me, but Veronica is making an effort, so why can't she? Maybe I'll have the chance to talk to her later on.

We all take seats on the balcony and get comfortable. The boys stay on their side, both of them looking out towards the harbour, drinking their beers. I wish Levi was here to spend the night not only with me, but with them as well. If it meant he was here, I'd share him, and it makes me sad that we're having fun, or at least trying to, without him.

Veronica brings some food out, and we sit and watch the boats on the harbour. It really is a great view, and despite Levi not being here, I'm actually looking forward to seeing the fireworks tonight. I've never come into the city to see them. Usually I'm home on the lounge watching the nine pm fireworks, then I fall into bed minutes after the second round ends at midnight. I'm actually excited about seeing them up close and in person, and getting to hear them, instead of listening to the bangs filtered through the TV.

Veronica cranks the music, and I'm happy to sit and listen, watching people walk around below, getting ready and finding places to sit for the night.

"Thank you," I say to Veronica. "For ..." I wave my hand, "... all this."

"No worries, bitch." She grins, and I laugh.

For a few hours we sit and talk, listen to music, watch

the harbour, eat food, and drink. I pace myself, but by quarter to nine, some of the others haven't been as careful.

Rachel is a sleepy, giggly drunk, and with fifteen minutes until the first round of fireworks, I figure now is a good time to talk to her. She gets up to go inside for another drink, and I follow. I make myself look busy grabbing some food from the table. Rachel sways on her feet as she pours herself another glass of champagne.

"You want some food as well?" I ask, filling a bowl with a fresh packet of chips.

"Okay." She smiles.

I look at her for a few seconds then open my mouth, but I have no idea what to say. She's so different to me, and I feel inadequate somehow, like I'm not good enough to be standing next to her.

I hold the chips out to her. "Here you go."

"Thanks." She sticks her hand in and stuffs some food in her mouth.

I follow Rachel back to the balcony, shaking my head at myself, and plonk into a seat beside Karen. *That was successful.*

"What's the matter?" Karen asks.

"Huh? Nothing, why?"

"Your face is all screwed up." Karen gestures with her hand.

I flick my gaze towards Rachel then lower my voice. "Just … thought I could talk to her, you know. And … nothing."

"Don't sweat it." Karen pinches a chip from my hand.

"Two minutes," Geoff calls from the boys' balcony.

Those who are sitting get up, and we all try to squish

together along the balcony rail. There's not enough room for six of us. Jessica is beside me so I grab her hand and pull her inside.

"There's more room next door," I say.

She follows me through to the adjoining suite, and we go onto the balcony with the boys. Geoff looks at me sideways, and Jarred frowns, but I'm not sure if it's aimed at me or Jessica.

Soon, the sky is filled with bursts of colour in red, blue, yellow, and white. I grip the railing and tilt my head back, taking it all in. Bangs echo over the harbour. The murmur of traffic and voices drift up from below, drowned out with every new explosion. A light breeze pushes my hair away from my face, and I smile. For a moment I'm lost in the fireworks display. My mind is blank, and I concentrate on the beauty of it all. Then the last sparks fall, and I'm pulled back to reality.

I glance at Jessica beside me. She's staring at the water, her eyes glistening.

Geoff pushes off the railing and sits at the small table. "I hope the midnight show is better than that."

"It always is," Jessica whispers beside me.

Jarred frowns, and looks at Jessica before going to sit with Geoff. Something is going on between them, but I have no idea what. It's as if Jarred is angry at her for something. Why would he be though? Jessica hasn't done anything to anyone.

I lean into her, gently nudging her shoulder. "Midnight will be awesome. You know, I've never seen the New Year's fireworks up close."

"It's been a couple of years since I have," Jessica says.

"The last time was with Josie. Mum and Dad let us come to the city on our own." A tear slips down her cheek and she swipes it away.

"I remember that," I say. "I wanted to come with you, but I wasn't allowed."

Jessica takes a shaky breath, and she puts her head on my shoulder. "I miss her."

"I know." I put my arm around her shoulders

"It's my fault she's dead."

"Don't be silly. It was an accident," I say. "You weren't even there."

"I'm the reason she was out."

Jarred scoffs from the table. When I look at him, he shakes his head, and takes a long draw from his beer. He stares at me over the top of his can.

"It's still not your fault," I say.

Jarred gets up and goes inside.

"The last thing I said to her was ..." Jessica's breathing hitches. "I called her a bitch, Katie." She pulls away from me and grips the railing, turning towards the lights of the bridge so I can't see her face.

"Hey, what're you doing over there?" Karen calls from the other balcony. "Come back. We have more food."

"Hang on," I call. I touch Jessica's elbow. "You didn't mean it. Josie loved you, and she'd hate to see you like this. Let's go eat something. You might feel better with food in your stomach."

She turns back to me and nods. I follow her through the door into the suite. Jarred immediately goes outside to the balcony again. *What is going on?*

I glance at my friend then out to Jarred. "What's up

with him?"

Jessica opens her mouth to speak, then snaps it shut again. She shakes her head and takes a quick look at Jarred. "Nothing. Don't worry about it."

"Okay, but you know you can talk to me, yeah?"

Jessica smiles with pursed lips. "Of course."

We go next door to where the other girls are gathered around the small dining table. It's covered with open pizza boxes, and my stomach rumbles.

"More champagne," Rachel cries, grabbing three slices of pizza and her full glass before going out to the balcony.

Veronica rolls her eyes. "I have a feeling I'll be picking her up off the floor soon." She takes a slice, following Rachel.

Jessica puts a slice of pizza on a napkin. She sits on the couch, squishing herself into the corner and tucking her legs underneath herself.

"Jess okay?" Karen whispers before stuffing her mouth with food.

I shake my head. "She still thinks Josie dying is her fault. And there's something going on with Jarred. He's … acting weird and broody around her."

"Jess said she had a huge fight with Josie the night she died." Stacey glances over at our friend on the couch. "She won't give me any details though."

"Daniel said she told him the same thing, but no details either," I say.

"She'll talk to us when she's ready." Karen picks up her glass. "I'm getting a refill."

Stacey and I do the same, and we spend the next couple of hours sipping our drinks, eating too much food, and watching the world go by out on the harbour. Rachel falls asleep in a chair around a quarter to twelve.

"She's going to miss the fireworks," Stacey says.

"If I hadn't switched to vodka and Coke, I think I'd miss them, too." Karen looks at us with droopy eyes.

"We should draw on her face," Veronica says.

"I'll get a pen." I giggle and jump up from my seat. The balcony moves, and I stumble a step, giggling again.

"You're drunk," Karen says.

I straighten. "Am not." But when I go to walk it's not as easy as it should be.

"Hurry up and come back. The fireworks are on soon. And get Jess out here."

I go inside, the pen forgotten, but Jessica isn't on the lounge where she's been since dinner. I glance around, then shuffle towards the bedroom. Maybe she went to sleep.

"Katie, come on," Stacey calls. "Five minutes."

I open one bedroom door and flick the light on, but Jessica isn't in there. I check the other bedroom, but she's not in there either. Then I hear voices. Someone yells, but I can't make out the words. My head is a little fuzzy from all the champagne, even though I've tried to pace myself, but I feel happy and floaty. I pull the bedroom door closed.

"Katie!" Karen calls. "Hurry up."

Voices sound again.

The door to the adjoining suite is slightly open, and I walk towards it. Maybe Jessica went next door to talk to the boys. The voices get louder, and when I reach the door I can finally make out the words.

"What you did was a low move," Jarred says. "You deserve everything you get."

I suck in a breath. *What did Jessica do?*

"Katie!" Karen yells again. "Countdown is on."

Voices chant in the background. *Seven, six, five …* but I block them out.

I grip the edge of the door and pull it open.

Fireworks explode. Karen and the girls on the balcony behind me cheer. Bursts of colour flash through the sky. The combination of loud voices and banging hurts my head.

"I'm so sorry." Jessica stands in the middle of the sitting room, tears coursing down her cheeks, the fireworks making them glow.

Jarred has his back to me, his fists clenched at his sides. "Tell that to your dead sister."

I quickly glance around the room. Geoff is on the balcony, leaning his forearms on the railing. His head hangs as if he's staring down at the ground.

"I thought you knew it was me," Jessica says.

"I did, eventually, but …" Jarred grips his hair with one hand. "I expected you to stop."

What the hell happened?"

"Then how can you blame me if you knew?" Jessica steps towards Jarred, her face crumpled. I've never heard her raise her voice like this.

"Because you're the one who agreed to the dare," Jarred yells.

Oh no. There was another dare? What was Jessica dared to do? Who dared her? Do I want to know? Whatever it was, Josephine wound up dead because of it.

Fuck! Everything comes back to that stupid game.

8

Thick and fast

I stand in the doorway staring at Jessica and Jarred. Fireworks continue to explode behind them. Neither of them has seen me—they're too fixated on glaring at each other.

"Katie?" Karen says at my side. "You missed the countdown. What's going on?"

Jessica's gaze meets mine, and she swipes the tears from her cheeks. I go into the room, not answering Karen. Jessica's sister died, and Levi ended up in the hospital.

Because of a dare.

"I can't believe you're still playing that game!" I yell. "What happened, Jess?"

She closes her eyes and cries harder. I want to comfort her, because she's my friend and she's hurting, but after what I went through with Levi, why would she have agreed to play?

Geoff comes in from the balcony and stands in the doorway, his face marred with a deep frown.

Jarred turns around and faces me. "Josie should never have been in that car." Then he grabs his keys off the coffee table and heads for the door.

"Jarred, stop," I say.

Has he been drinking? We've all been drinking. He can't drive if he's been drinking. Does he have his car here? Why would he bring his car to the city? So many questions fill my head in seconds, and my mind goes fuzzy.

"What?" he asks.

"Don't drive," I say. "Don't … don't drink and drive."

Jarred picks up a backpack that's sitting beside the dining table. He doesn't respond with anything more than a small nod, then he leaves.

Geoff runs a hand down his face. Then he lashes out at the wall beside him, punching it. He leaves a red smear on the rendered concrete.

"This is so fucked up." He grabs his stuff and follows Jarred.

"What's happening in here?" Stacey asks from the doorway to the other suite.

"I have no idea." Karen throws her hands in the air and sits on the couch.

"Jess?" Stacey walks towards her. "What happened?"

Jessica's shoulders heave, and she shakes her head, looking down at her feet. "Can we go home?" Her voice is barely a whisper. "I can't do this anymore." She drops to her knees, then lies down and curls into a ball.

"How about we get you to bed," Stacey says, kneeling

beside her. "The boys are gone so we can sleep in here. Tomorrow will be better, I promise. And we can go home first thing." Stacey helps Jessica to her feet and they start towards one of the bedrooms. "We'll see you all in the morning." They go in and close the door.

"Well ..." Karen gets to her feet. "I think this party's over. I'm going to bed, too." She raises her eyebrows at me, and I'm pretty sure she wants me to go with her so we can talk about what the hell is going on.

I follow her back into our suite. Rachel is still outside, asleep in the chair. Veronica is sitting at the dining table, picking at the leftover food.

"Sounded intense in there," she says. "I didn't want to interrupt."

"Jarred and Geoff left," I say. "Jarred's pretty pissed at Jess. Something about her doing a dare, and that's why Levi and Josie had their accident. You know anything about that?"

"If you think I had anything to do with it, then you're wrong." Veronica sits up straight in her chair.

"Who did then?" Karen asks. "And what the hell was she dared to do?"

Veronica stares at both of us and sighs. "The day we all came home from Surfers, Josie dared Jess to twin swap with her."

"Why would she do that?" I ask. "And why were you even playing truth or dare in the first place?"

"We weren't. It was more of a spur-of-the-moment thing." Veronica munches on a pizza crust. "None of us knew about it. Josie wanted to see if they could pull it off. If any of us would notice. Apparently, they switched at the airport up there. Then Jess came with us, and Josie went home with Stacey."

"That's crazy," Karen says, dropping into a seat at the table. "Did it work?"

"Mostly … It took me a while, but Josie is … was … one of my closest friends. By the time we landed in Sydney, I knew it was Jess with us." Veronica glances outside at Rachel asleep in the chair. "Rach is too caught up in herself to notice anything. Ever."

I rub my temples, trying to get my thoughts around what Veronica is telling us. Too much champagne has made my head ache. Jessica and Josephine twin swapped? They've done it before, but one of them must have done something bad for them to have had a huge fight after. I sit at the table next to Karen.

"Then what happened?" Karen asks, leaning towards Veronica.

"Josie and Stacey were on a different flight to ours, so Jess went home with Jarred. Josie called me when she got home. She said Stacey was clueless, and she wanted to know if I'd figured it out, but she also asked where Jess was." Veronica shrugs. "I told her she went with Jarred. I don't know what went down after that. The twins obviously fought about something big though, and my money is on Jess and Jarred …" Veronica bites her lip, makes an O with the thumb and finger on her left hand, then moves her right index finger in and out of it.

"No," I say. "Jess would never do that to her sister."

Veronica shrugs again. "I guess we'll never know unless she tells one of us."

I shake my head. "This is so messed up."

"Yeah," Karen says beside me. "I think I need to sleep now. Too much excitement for one night."

Sleep is probably what we all need. Rachel already seems pretty comfortable out on the balcony. Veronica gets up and stumbles out there, shaking Rachel's shoulder until she stirs. She helps her friend inside and they disappear into the first bedroom. I grab my bag and go to the bathroom to wash my face and take my contacts out, then Karen and I crawl under the covers of the double bed in the second bedroom.

"I hope Jess didn't do what Veronica thinks she did," Karen says. She lies on her side, facing me, and tucks her hand under her head.

"I hope so, too." I sigh.

"Happy New Year." Karen blows me a kiss then rolls over.

I lie on my back and stare at the ceiling, wishing I was in my own bed. Within minutes, Karen is snoring softly. I close my eyes and try to sleep, but my mind is racing with too many thoughts, and I open them again.

Why did Josephine want to twin swap with Jessica? Why did Jessica agree? If they hadn't done any of this, would Josephine still be alive? Would Levi never have hit her car?

I squeeze my eyes shut and pinch the bridge of my nose. When did everything become so messed up? At what point did my life, and the lives of my friends, start to fall apart? If one event changed, or didn't happen at all, would we be somewhere else right now?

What if Josephine didn't die?

What if Levi was fine?

What if everything had happened differently?
What if?

My brain goes over the past six months, over and over, each time remembering something different. I'm not sure how long I lie here unable to sleep. I think I drift off a few times, but my thoughts always bring me back.

Light seeps into the sky outside, and Karen stirs beside me. I feel like I've had no sleep, but the only thing I want to do is go home.

I carefully get out of bed, trying not to wake Karen, and use the bathroom before going onto the balcony to watch the sunrise. Jessica is sitting in a seat on the other balcony, slumped down with her feet up on the railing.

"You couldn't sleep either?" I ask, moving a chair so I can sit at the end closest to her.

She shakes her head. "I don't sleep much at all these days."

I let her voice drift out into the morning noise before I reply, "Do you want to talk about anything?"

Jessica looks over at me. Her eyes are rimmed with red. "I'm not sure I can get the words out and make any sense." She pauses, and her eyes go vacant. "None of it makes any sense."

"Maybe you should write it down. I find writing in my journal helps with a lot of stuff."

Jessica looks away again, gazing out towards the bridge. "Maybe."

We sit for a while, listening to the commotion below, and watch as the sun lights up the horizon. Its rays spread across the city, showering diamonds of light onto the harbour. For a moment I feel at peace, watching nature's beautiful display.

"Every day is a fresh start," I say, then I look over at Jessica. She takes a deep breath. "It has to be better than the last, right?"

"Who wants to go home?" Karen asks, coming onto the balcony and stretching.

"I think home sounds fantastic." I get up and put the chair back at the table. "Want to train it with us?" I ask Jessica.

She nods. "I'll have a shower, and see what Stacey's doing."

We're all a bit slow this morning, and by the time we've had our showers, packed our stuff, helped Veronica clean up a bit, and thanked her, the four of us don't make it home until almost lunchtime.

Karen and I say goodbye to Stacey and Jessica at the station, then walk back to Karen's place before jumping in the car to go to mine.

"How was your night?" Mum washes some lettuce in the colander, then wipes her hands on a towel before facing us. Karen and I sit at the kitchen bench.

"All right," I say.

"The fireworks were awesome," Karen adds.

"You didn't get up to too much mischief I hope." Mum smiles, then turns back to the chopping board. "What are your plans for the rest of the day?"

I lean my elbows on the counter, and rest my chin on my hand. "Going to see Levi."

Mum puts down the knife she's been using to cut the tomatoes. "Maybe you should go over your uni letters and decide what you're going to do. You don't have long until final enrolment is due."

I sit up straight in my seat. "Maybe … I was thinking I could take a year off."

"A year off what?" Dad asks, coming into the kitchen from outside.

"Everything," I say. "Defer for a year."

"In order for you to defer, you have to make a decision about which university you're going to attend," Mum says, putting her hands on her hips. "And the answer is no. You're not taking a year off."

Karen is quiet beside me, and I bet she's wishing she wasn't here.

I stare at my hands, and twist my fingers together. "Jess is going to."

"You're not Jessica," Dad says. "You haven't been through what she has."

No, but my life hasn't been a walk in the park either.

"Katie, you've worked so hard," Mum says. "Don't throw it away now."

"You think all my hard work equals a high profile career as a lawyer or a doctor?" I ask.

"Well, yes." Mum folds her arms over her chest. "And if you take a year off you'll be twelve months behind."

"I don't want to study law. And after what happened with Levi and Josie, there's no way I'm doing medicine." I jump up from my seat.

Dad comes around the counter to stand beside Mum. "Tell us what you want to do, honey."

"I want to do a fine arts degree, and I applied at SCA as my first choice above everything else. But I haven't received a letter from them."

Mum presses her lips into a thin line. She drops her gaze from mine, then walks past me to the sideboard in the dining room. She comes back with an envelope in her hand and passes it to me.

I take it from her, trying to read her expression. When I look down at the envelope, it has the Sydney College of the Arts logo on it.

The letter I've been waiting for.

I turn the letter over. It's been opened. I shake my head and pull the paper out. I've been accepted, but when I read further, I've missed the interview cut-off date.

"Why didn't you give this to me?" I look up at Mum. "It's my life. You had no right!"

I throw the letter onto the bench and storm out, grabbing my tote bag on my way to the front door. I'm tired of trying to live up to everyone's expectations. Why can't I make my own decisions?

The sun is hot on my face as I run across the front yard to the road. I really wish I had my own car—then I could go anywhere I wanted to. But instead I have to rely on everyone else for everything.

"Arrrgggghhh!" I scream at the sky and stamp my foot.

Josephine is dead.

One of my closest friends is falling apart.

Levi is still in hospital.

And my parents are trying to control my life.

I just want to run away from everything.

I adjust the strap of my tote bag on my shoulder, hang my toes off the edge of the kerb, and look up the street.

"Want a lift somewhere?" Karen asks.

I turn to my best friend. "Can you take me to the

hospital, if it's not too much trouble?"

Karen comes over and puts an arm around my shoulders. "Nothing for you is ever too much trouble. Get in."

I slide into the front passenger seat and buckle my belt. Mum is standing at the front door as we pull away from the kerb. I'll have to face her and Dad again later, but hopefully I'll have calmed down by then.

"They'll come around," Karen says, turning onto the highway.

"It's not that," I say. "It's too late anyway. I've missed the interview, so I'll have to settle for one of the other unis."

"You shouldn't settle for anything."

I shrug and stare out the window the rest of the trip, not really in the mood to talk about it with Karen. I want to tell Levi what's happened, even if he doesn't talk back.

Karen parks the car on the street outside the hospital. "Want me to come with?"

"Do you want to?"

She smiles. "I know you probably have a lot you want to tell him."

"Yeah, but I like having you around."

"Let's go then."

We get out of the car and take the familiar walk into the hospital and to the ICU. I use the phone at the door, and the nurse at the desk lets us in. When we reach Levi's room, he already has visitors. Jessica is standing next to Levi's bed with Daniel at her side. As far as I know, it's the first time Jessica has come to the hospital.

"Hi girls," Yvonne says, coming over from the water fountain.

"Hi." I turn to her. "Happy New Year. How is he?"

"Since yesterday? Not much change." She looks through the window at her son. "But they say he should be fully conscious any day now."

I look through the window, too. "When did Daniel and Jess get here?"

"Not long ago," Yvonne says. "Maybe ten minutes?"

Daniel wasn't home when we were there, so he must have met up with Jessica and brought her straight here.

"Jess … is she … Are you okay with …" I stop and take a breath, looking at Yvonne. "You don't mind her being here?"

Yvonne smiles. "No, sweetie. Of course not. I hope seeing Levi helps her somehow. I know she's been struggling."

Yeah, she has. I turn back to the window.

Daniel puts an arm around Jessica's shoulders, but she shrugs him free. She turns with the movement, and I can see the profile of her face. She's crying really hard, and her chest heaves. Daniel reaches for her again, but she steps back, shaking her head.

"What's going on in there?" Karen asks. "Jess is pretty upset."

"I'll go and see." Yvonne steps around us and opens the door.

"It's all my fault," Jessica screams, her voice piercing the relative quiet of the ICU.

Yvonne takes a few hurried steps forward. "Jess, honey, calm down."

I catch the door before it closes, stopping at the threshold. The rules are only two visitors at a time in Levi's room. There are already three people in there. Karen and I aren't supposed to go in.

"You don't understand," Jessica yells, tears streaming down her cheeks. "It's my fault. I killed my sister. I killed her." She shoves her hands into her hair and pulls, letting out a strangled cry filled with heartache and pain.

I want to go to her, and hold her, and tell her everything will be all right. Yvonne whispers to Jessica in hushed tones, so low I can't make out the words. With a motherly touch, she manages to untangle Jessica's hands from her hair. Karen presses into my side and we both fill the doorway.

"What's happening?" a nurse asks from behind us, but neither of us turn around.

Daniel reaches out to Jessica and pulls her to his chest. She doesn't resist this time, going to him easily. She sobs into his shirt, and he gently moves her away from the bed.

My gaze follows them, then I look at Levi.

My heart skips.

I try to move, but my feet are like lead bricks.

"Levi!" I cry.

He turns his head slowly, and finally I get to look into his eyes.

"Katie?" he asks. "Mum …? Where am I?"

Yvonne rushes to his side.

Then I stumble into the room, my tears coming thick and fast.

9

My escape

A nurse shoulders past me, and then a doctor and another nurse come into the room.

"Everyone, out," the female nurse says. "There are too many people in here." She gets between me and Levi, and I want to shove her out of the way.

Daniel pulls Jessica towards me. She's still sobbing and trying to get words out.

"Levi, I'm sorry," she says, struggling in Daniel's arms. "It's my fault. It should've been me … My fault … Josie …" She wails, and Daniel manages to get her out the door.

Karen grabs my arm and pulls me back.

"Levi." I try to shake my best friend off and push forward.

"You can talk to him later," the nurse says, forcing me back towards the door. "Right now we need to check him over and keep him calm. You being here isn't helping."

I stumble out of the room and the door is shut in my face. I run to the window, aware of Karen at my side, but I ignore her, too intent on watching Levi through the glass. I press my palm to the cool surface, and search for his face behind the bodies of the medical staff. The doctor leans over him, and the nurses fuss around the machines.

Yvonne is still in the room. She stands back and to the side, a hand covering her mouth. Jessica sobs behind me, and I look over my shoulder at my brother.

He frowns. "Come on, Jess." He rests his chin on top of her head and stares at me. "I'll take you home." Daniel leads her away, and I turn back to the window.

"He'll be okay," Karen says, rubbing my back.

"I want to talk to him." I press my forehead to the glass. "I *need* to talk to him."

A nurse opens the door and comes out.

"Katie?" Levi calls.

"Levi!" I yell.

His lips move and form my name again. "Katie …" He struggles to sit up in bed, but the doctor puts a firm hand on his shoulder and pushes him back.

One of the nurses goes to the drip beside his bed and inserts a syringe into the line. *What are they doing?* I run back to the door and open it, but I'm quickly stopped by the same nurse who forced me out of the room.

"You can't be in here," she says.

"I want to talk to him." I sniffle and stare at her with wide eyes.

"Not yet. He needs to be calm."

Yvonne comes over, and I step back onto the ward. She closes the door behind her, leaving the nurse on the other side. Leaving Levi on the other side.

"Maybe it's best if you come back tomorrow," Yvonne says. My eyes fill with more tears, and everything blurs. She reaches out and rubs my arm. "The doctors say he's under too much stress now that he's fully awake. Everyone being here has made it worse. He can't make any sudden movements." Yvonne looks at me with sympathetic eyes. "Once he's had time to adjust, and I can explain to him what's happened, I think it's best if no one else is here. I don't know what he remembers. If he remembers anything at all. Okay?"

I nod, and suck in a deep breath, letting it out shakily. "I can see him tomorrow?"

"Yes, I'm sure tomorrow will be fine." Yvonne smiles, but her eyes are sad.

"Come on, Katie." Karen leans gently against my shoulder. "I'll drive you home."

Reluctantly, I follow Karen out of the ICU to where we parked the car on the street. I've been waiting for this day since we got back from schoolies—for Levi to finally wake up. Now that it's happened, I can't even talk to him. I have so much to tell him, and so many lost days to make up for.

I get in the car and dump my tote at my feet, leaning my head back against the car seat and closing my eyes. I hope Karen doesn't want to talk on the way home, because I can't. I'm not sure my voice will work without cracking. How can I wait until tomorrow to see Levi?

Tomorrow may never come.

The thought scares me, and I have to take deep breaths to calm myself down.

"Everything all right?" Karen asks as we turn off the highway towards my place. "You look like you're having a panic attack."

I open my eyes and turn to her. "I want to talk to him, Karen. What if something happens and I never get to do that? Tomorrow is so far away. What if—"

"Stop," she says. "Don't do that. If you go there, you'll go crazy. I know life is short, and we've all learnt that first hand recently, but you can't think like that." She pulls into my driveway and turns the car off. "You have to keep believing that tomorrow will come, and it will be better than today."

I nod, and then the tears come again. My shoulders shake as I try to hold them back, but then I let out a sob that rattles my chest and makes my heart ache.

"Oh, sweetie, come here." Karen reaches over and wraps her arms around me. She rubs my back while I cry, and we sit like that for a couple of minutes before she says, "I should get home. You going to be okay?"

I sniffle and pull away. "Yeah, I'm good."

Mum's car is in the driveway, which means she's home, and I remember our argument this morning about uni, and me running out. I squeeze my eyes closed for a second, then get out of the car and walk to the front door, waving to Karen when I reach the step. I hope Mum's not on the defensive, because I'm not in the mood for another fight. When I get inside, she comes out of the lounge room and meets me at the bottom of the stairs.

"Daniel said Levi's awake." She looks at me and waits. I nod. "Oh, honey, that's great news." She wraps me up in a hug, and it feels better than any hug I've had in the past few weeks, because it's Mum. "I'm sorry about this morning." She strokes my hair.

I pull away. "Can we talk about it later? I'm … My mind is elsewhere. They wouldn't let me talk to Levi. I can't go back until tomorrow."

"Sure, honey. We'll work it out." Mum smiles. "Do you want something to eat?"

"I'd like to go over to the treehouse first," I say. "I want to write in my journal."

Mum presses her lips together. "Don't be too long."

I adjust the strap of my tote on my shoulder and go back outside, cross over to Levi's yard, and walk down the side of the house.

Up in the treehouse, I sit on the floor, take my journal and a pen out, then settle against the wall, feeling comfortable in this space where Levi and I share so many good memories.

Levi woke up today. I guess I couldn't ask for a better New Year's present, except they wouldn't let me in the room, so I couldn't talk to him. My head understands the reasons, but my heart doesn't. I've been waiting to hear his voice for so long, and now I know he's awake, it's torture not being able to be by his side.

Tomorrow.

If tomorrow ever comes.

Karen told me off for thinking like that, but after everything that's happened, I'm scared. I'm scared of losing him again.

I put my pen down, because I'm not sure what else to write. Mum said not to be too long, but I don't want to go back yet. I like the quiet up here. Levi's box of letters is still in the corner, and I want to read another one, but guilt settles into my stomach, making it churn.

I argue with myself for a few minutes before reaching under the table and pulling the box out. I reason again that the letters have my name on them, so it should be okay for me to read them. This time, I decide to read the most recent one. The letter that Levi wrote the day he came home from schoolies. The day Josephine died.

Dear Katie,

I just got back from schoolies, and I can't wait for you to get home tomorrow. I bet if you were to read this you'd be able to imagine the smile in my voice. I'm not sure if you ever will though … read this, that is. Because I've never had enough courage to give you any of the letters I've written you. Maybe I will soon, because I do want you to read them. All of them.

But that's not what I wanted to write down.

I wanted to write down how excited I am about everything! You and me. Our future. Hopefully, we have one together.

I've learnt a lot of stuff about you, and about myself. I've realised what's most important, and it's not money, or possessions, or what other people think … it's all the things that money can't buy.

Sunlight on your hair.

How your mouth is a little lopsided when you smile.

The warmth of your hand in mine.

So many things that matter more than anything else. All the little things that add up to make the big picture so much brighter.

I'm sorry for everything I've put you through. I hope you've forgiven me, because when you get home, I want to hold you and never let you go.

I have so much to tell you about everything. So many things I want to share with you that until now I've been too afraid to say out loud.

Today is the last day of our past.

Tomorrow is the first day of the rest of our lives.

I love you.

Levi x

With a sad smile, I fold the paper again and slip it back into the envelope. The first day of the rest of our lives didn't work out how we expected it to, but now that Levi is awake, maybe we have another chance. I hope he remembers writing this, but what if he doesn't? What if he doesn't remember anything? I've heard of that happening to patients who have been in serious accidents or suffered extensive trauma.

I need to talk to him.

I pull my legs to my chest, and wrap my arms around them, closing my eyes and resting my forehead on my knees. With a few deep breaths, I try to steady the shake creeping into my shoulders. Knowing Levi is awake but not being able to go and see him is torture.

I concentrate on breathing evenly, keeping my eyes closed. I listen to the world outside the treehouse, the birds chirping and the rustle of the summer breeze through the gum trees.

Then a voice breaks the serenity.

I can't understand the words, but they sound angry,

with an abrupt edge.

The voice becomes clearer, and I raise my head, staring out through the gaps in the leaves of the tree.

Mark and Yvonne are standing on the back deck. From where I'm sitting, I can see straight into the top level of the house. If either of them glanced over at the treehouse, they could probably make me out in the shadows. I move to the other wall where the curtains are, and crouch beside the table, hoping that the piece of torn fabric and the dimness of the late afternoon light is enough to hide me from their sight.

"I don't want you there," Yvonne yells.

Mark's fists are clenched. "He's my son."

"I don't care." Yvonne crosses her arms, and looks at her feet. "You've done enough damage to this family already."

"Don't you talk to me like that."

I shouldn't be listening to their conversation. It's none of my business.

"It's about time I stood up to you," Yvonne says.

Mark raises his hand.

I hold my breath.

Yvonne stands her ground, but she leans away, her shoulders hunched to her ears.

Mark slaps Yvonne across the cheek, and her head whips to the side.

My hand flies to my mouth, and I squeeze my eyes shut, but tears still make their way out of the corners.

He hit her!

A door slams.

Slowly, I open my eyes, my vision blurry and my hand still over my mouth.

I blink a few times.

Yvonne is now alone on the back deck, her arms wrapped around herself as she cries.

I've known Levi and his family my entire life. Mark has often seemed angry and unapproachable, and I've been suspicious of him hitting Levi in the past, but I have never *seen* Mark raise a hand to his wife or his kids.

I want to un-see it.

What am I supposed to do?

When I told Mum I was worried about Levi, she just told me to be there for him. How do I do that? How do I help someone who has potentially been abused by his father? I don't know what it's like. And what about Yvonne? I don't know how to deal with this.

Levi shouldn't *have* to deal with this.

Maybe I should have paid more attention. Were there more signs? Should I have been able to tell this was going on? I can't rush in accusing Mark of abuse when I don't know any facts.

I hug my knees and rock back and forth, waiting for Yvonne to go inside so I can get out of here and go home. She stands at the railing of the deck, staring out towards the view of the bush I know is behind me. I hug my knees tighter, and try to make myself as small as possible so she doesn't see me.

A car starts out the front, and Yvonne moves to the back door. I hold my breath. She finally goes inside, the sliding door clicking closed behind her. As quickly and quietly as I can, I climb down the treehouse steps and race across the backyard, making my escape.

Together again?

I don't sleep well, worried about what I saw and what I should do about it. It's really none of my business, but what if Yvonne needs help? What if Levi does, too? How can I live with knowing what I know, and not say something to someone?

I'm quiet at breakfast, with so many things rushing through my head. Soon I'll get to talk to Levi for the first time in what feels like forever.

"Katie?" Mum says. "Katie, did you hear me?"

"Huh?" I drop my spoon into my bowl of cereal.

"What's the matter? You're a million miles away."

I shrug. "Just thinking."

"I can see that." Mum stands on the kitchen side of the counter and crosses her arms. "I said, we need to talk about uni tonight when I get home from work."

111

I look down at my bowl and my half-eaten cereal. "I already told you, I don't want to do law."

"I know, honey. Just …" She sighs. "We'll talk tonight. I need to get going."

I nod, and she comes around the counter to give me a kiss.

"Mum?" I say as she reaches the door. "If you knew something about someone, and it wasn't very good, like they were hurting someone you loved, would you step in? Would you say something?" I bite my lip and stare at her. "Would you get involved when you know it's none of your business?"

Mum smiles at me, but her eyes are sad. "Sometimes it's best not to get too involved. But if someone I loved was getting hurt, I would do whatever I could to help." She looks at me for another moment, and I get the feeling she's about to ask who I'm talking about, but then she comes over and gives me a hug. "Say hi to Levi for me today, okay?"

I nod and bury my face in her chest, hugging her back. She pulls away then leaves for work, and I'm left in the empty kitchen to think about what to do. Dad left early, and Daniel is sleeping because he worked the late shift, so I have no one else to talk to.

I go upstairs to my room and get ready to go to the hospital. I haven't worn my contacts much lately, but today I want to make the effort. Because it has been a while it takes me a little longer to get them in, and by the time I'm done my eyes are watering and a sick feeling has settled into my stomach.

Or maybe it's because I know I'm eventually going to

have to ask Levi about his dad.

If I don't, I'm a terrible friend.

But if I do, will it make it worse?

I stare at my reflection in the mirror, and take a second to be grateful for my parents and how wonderful they are. I've had it tough in other ways, but Mum and Dad having big dreams for me is a very different kind of torture compared to being physically abused by the people who are supposed to protect us. My parents have always loved each other, and Daniel and me.

I take my time brushing my hair, letting my eyes settle while I do, then I put a little bit of gloss on my lips. I grab my tote, making sure my phone, purse, and journal are in there, then I go out to the front yard to wait for Karen. I turn my face to the summer sun and let it warm my cheeks. I hear a door open, and Yvonne steps onto the front veranda next door. She waves, and I wave back, offering her a smile as well.

Yvonne comes down the steps and onto the path. "I'm going to the hospital, Katie. Would you like to come with me today?"

"Oh, thank you, but I'm waiting for Karen."

Seconds later a car comes over the rise.

"All right. I'll see you both there." She smiles as Karen pulls up to the kerb. "Levi is looking forward to seeing you. He wouldn't stop asking for you yesterday."

I study Yvonne's face for a few heartbeats, trying to see if there's any evidence of Mark's assault yesterday. There doesn't seem to be—on the surface.

"Does he … is he …" I tuck my hair behind my ear. "Does he remember what happened?"

Yvonne takes a deep breath. "His memory of before the accident is fine, but he seems to have lost a little bit of time. He doesn't remember the accident, or why he was driving in the first place."

I nod. "Okay, so I can … talk to him about Josie? Does he know …?"

"Yes, sweetie. I told him what happened to Josie."

I nod again. "Okay."

Yvonne heads to her car. "See you soon."

I wait until she's out of the driveway and up the road before getting into the car.

"All set?" Karen asks.

I take a deep, shaky breath. "Yeah, I'm nervous though."

"Don't be. It's Levi. I'll bet he can't wait to see you."

I don't reply, because seeing Levi isn't the only thing I'm nervous about. It's also what I want to talk to him about that's making me shaky. But I'm not going to say anything to Karen until after I talk to Levi. I'm sure he wouldn't want me airing his dirty laundry. I don't know how to even start the conversation with him. *Hey, I was just wondering if your dad hits you and your mum. Want to talk to me about that?* How do I be tactful without sounding … not tactful?

"Earth to Katie," Karen says when we're almost at the hospital.

"Huh?" I turn to her.

"You zoned out."

"Sorry, just … thinking." I tell her what I told Mum when she caught me in my own world at breakfast.

Karen parks the car and gets out. I follow, crossing the street to the front entrance of the hospital. The walk along the corridor feels different this morning, like I'm doing it for the first time, and when we reach the doors to the ICU, my hands are shaking and I can hardly pick up the phone.

Karen rubs my arm. "Calm down. Deep breaths."

After we wash our hands one of the nurses lets us in, and we make our way to Levi's room. Yvonne is with him, and Karen and I stop at the window. I look in, waiting for him to adjust his gaze and see us. When he does, his eyes light up, and a smile spreads across his face. I can't help smiling as well.

Yvonne turns, then gets up from the chair beside the bed, coming to the door. I meet her at the threshold, eager to go in.

"I'll wait out here," Karen says. "Actually, I'll go get us some hot chocolate."

"Thank you," I say.

Yvonne holds the door and I walk into the room. "I'll go with Karen," she says.

I watch the door close, then I turn to Levi. I'm itching to run at him and hug him so tight, but I'm not sure if he's in any pain. It takes all my effort to walk normally to the side of the bed.

"You're a sight for sore eyes," Levi says.

I drop my tote on the floor, then my shoulders start to shake. I can't hold myself together anymore, and the tears course down my cheeks. I'm crying because I'm happy and sad all at the same time.

Levi lifts his hand and holds it out to me. The bed railing is down now, so I don't have to reach through it. I take his hand, and it feels so warm in mine as he gives me a gentle squeeze.

"Welcome back," I say through my tears. "I've been waiting so long to hear your voice."

"Don't cry." He pulls my hand.

I lean forward, then look him up and down. "Can I … hug you? I don't want to hurt you."

Levi smiles, and pulls my hand again. I reach around him with my other arm and lay my head on his chest, careful not to put too much weight on him. The wires and pads under his hospital gown are hard under my cheek.

For a few moments, I listen to the beating of Levi's heart and count his breaths with the rise and fall of his chest. I squeeze my eyes closed, and breathe in time with him.

"How are you feeling?" I finally ask, pulling away and straightening up.

"I'm sore in places I didn't know I had, but I'm okay." He smiles. "The doctors say I've healed well. My lung and ribs are good, but I'll be tender for a while yet."

"When can you come home?"

"Now that I'm fully awake and handling the pain, they're going to move me to the ward tomorrow. After that, I'm not sure how long. A week or two?"

"It's too long," I say. "I want you to come home. We've already lost so much time."

"We have all the time in the world, Katie."

I shake my head and grip his hand. "No, we don't. We don't know what's going to happen tomorrow. Tomorrow might never come. I can't lose you, not again. I've just gotten you back. We have to … we have—"

"Shhh." Levi reaches up and cups my cheek with his free hand. "It's okay. I'm here now. I'm not going anywhere."

"We don't know ..." I sob and press my face into his warm palm, closing my eyes. "We don't know what the future holds," I whisper.

"My future holds you."

I open my eyes and stare at Levi. "I have so much I want to talk to you about. So many things ... I don't know where to start."

Levi smiles. "How about I go first? How's Jess? From what I remember yesterday, she was pretty upset. Is she coping? Is she ...?" Levi takes his palm from my cheek and looks at our entwined fingers. "You have to be there for her, Katie. I'm sure she needs her friends."

When he looks up at me again, there's a sadness in his eyes that speaks for every person who has ever lost a loved one. If I ever lost Daniel, I fear my eyes would be just as haunted.

"She's not doing so well," I say. "She blames herself for Josie's death."

Levi half-laughs. "She wasn't driving the car that killed her."

"And it wasn't your fault." I pull the chair as close to the bed as I can and sit, never letting go of Levi's hand. He rolls his head to the side on his pillow, and I continue, "I'm guessing you haven't spoken to Jarred, or Geoff. Or Veronica?"

He shakes his head.

I take a deep breath because it's all so messed up. Everything is messed up. "There was ... Josie and Jess ... they twin swapped on the way home from Surfers. Jess went home with Jarred. Something must have happened, because Jess and Josie had a big fight. I don't know what about, but Jess is beside herself and thinks it's all her fault. She had an argument with Jarred on New Year's. I … don't know how to help her."

"Just … be there, and hopefully that will help enough."

I adjust myself in my seat, trying to think of a way into a conversation with Levi about his dad. "How about you?" I ask instead. "How are you coping with …?"

"Josie's death?" Levi raises his eyebrows. "I'm trying not to think about it. I can't remember much of that night, so I don't know what happened. Mum said the police will come and talk to me in a few days to get my side of the story, but I have no idea what to tell them. My car smashed into hers, but I don't remember it." Levi shoves his free hand into his hair and closes his eyes. "Since I woke up, I've tried to remember even getting in the car. A small detail. Anything. But I can't. The last thing I remember is going out to the treehouse and …"

I wait for him to continue, but he doesn't.

"I've been spending some time in the treehouse since you've been in hospital." I twist a lock of hair around my finger and look down at the bed. "I found the box of letters."

I hold my breath and wait for the question I think is coming next, but Levi doesn't ask it.

"I was wondering how long it would take you," he says. "I've been hoping for a long time that you'd go to the treehouse, but you never did."

"Don't you want to know if I've read them?" I look up at him again, guilt stabbing me in the stomach.

"Do you want to read them?"

"Do you want me to?"

Levi goes quiet and holds my gaze. Eventually, he says, "I do, but to be honest, I never intended to give them to you. So … the decision is yours."

"Why did you write them if you never wanted me to read them?"

"Why do you write in your journal?" He smiles.

I chew my bottom lip. "I write stuff down because it helps me deal with it better."

Levi nods. "Yeah, it does. I so badly wanted to talk to you when I started writing those letters, but I couldn't just come and see you, so I wrote it down instead. You were a pretty good listener."

I lean on the side of the bed with both elbows and adjust my hold on Levi's hand. "I've read two of them so far … I feel really guilty about it, like I've invaded your privacy."

"It's okay. I don't mind. Which ones have you read?"

"The last one you wrote, after coming back from Surfers, and the first one. The one after Mason died." I go quiet for a moment before continuing. "I would've listened. If you came to me, I would've listened."

"I did come," he says. "But I managed to screw everything up."

I think back to that first night Levi climbed into my bedroom window. Was that his way of trying to talk to me? To tell me what was going on with him? Back then I just thought he was drunk and being an idiot.

"Maybe I didn't listen hard enough."

Levi shakes his head. "No, none of this is your fault." He pauses. "If you do decide to read any more of the letters, read the one from the day of Mason's funeral."

"Okay." I don't say any more on the subject of the letters. "Have you seen your dad?" I ask instead.

Levi hesitates, and a funny look passes over his face. "Not yet. He hasn't come ..."

I bite my lip, and try to think of the best way to word my next question. I open my mouth a couple of times to speak, but then close it again.

"What's wrong, Katie?" Levi asks. "You're doing that thing with your mouth where you look like a fish."

I smile at the memory of Levi telling me I looked like a fish the first night he climbed in my window again. I miss him climbing in my window.

"I want to ask you something," I eventually say. "But you don't have to answer, because I know it's none of my business."

"Shoot," Levi says. "You can ask me anything."

I hesitate, then open my mouth and blurt, "I ... is there ... is everything okay with your dad?"

Levi stares at me for a long moment, and my heart beats faster. I hold my breath, because I think I know what he's going to say. I've seen the evidence, but I don't want it to be true.

"My dad is ... you need to read the letter from the day of Mason's funeral." Levi looks down at our hands, across the room, back to our hands. He runs circles over my skin with his thumb. "Just promise me one thing." Levi finally connects his gaze with mine again. "Remember I'm a different person now. I have everything to live for. I have you."

I'm puzzled by his words, and what could be in his letter, but I nod my agreeance.

Karen and Yvonne return with the hot chocolates, and Levi's mum leaves Karen and I to talk to Levi for a bit longer. I tell him about what happened with Mum and my uni letters, and that I still haven't followed up with any of my acceptances because of everything that's been going on.

"Mum was going to bring my letters in today," Levi says. "She doesn't want me to miss the cut-off date."

"Surely they can make a special consideration for you if you do," Karen says. "It's not like you *could* reply before now."

Levi shrugs. "We'll see. It will all work out."

The nurses haven't enforced the two visitors rule today since Levi is awake, and Yvonne pops in and out. I'm grateful she's letting Karen and I have so much time with her son. After lunch though, a nurse comes in and says it's time for us to leave.

"Now that you no longer need heavy sedation, we'll be moving you out of the ICU soon, maybe even as early as tomorrow," she says to Levi. "The doctor wants me to give you a good check over, and see if you're up to getting out of bed."

I stand from the chair. "I'll come see you again tomorrow, okay?"

"I'd like that," Levi says, squeezing my hand.

I lean down to hug him, and Levi reaches up to touch my hair. I stop and look into his eyes. He caresses my cheek with his fingertips, then slips his hand behind my neck and gently pulls me to him. I close my eyes. His kiss is chaste and soft. When I pull away, heat lingers on my lips, and I want to kiss him again, but there are other people in the room.

His hand falls away from my neck and I straighten. "See you soon."

"I'll be here." He smiles.

Karen and I say goodbye to Yvonne on our way out and head home.

"Need another lift tomorrow?" Karen asks as I get out of the car.

"Thank you. If it's no trouble?" I lean down and look through the window. "But I can catch the train home."

"Whatever." Karen waves her hand and smiles. "We'll sort it out later."

I wait for her to pull onto the street before turning back to the house. I have an hour or so before Mum should be home from work, so instead of going inside I go over to Levi's yard and make my way to the treehouse.

Once I'm at the top, I settle in with my back against the wall and pull the box out, flicking to the letter from the day of Mason's funeral. I run my fingers over the outside of the envelope before pulling the contents out and reading.

Dear Katie,

Today was Mason's funeral, and it has been one of the hardest days of my life. I still can't believe Mason isn't here anymore. But him not being here isn't the only reason today was difficult.

When I saw you, I just wanted to come over and hug you, and tell you how much it meant to me that you were there. Having you near was so comforting, and it helped me get through the day when all I wanted to do was run.

Over the past week I've been thinking about how much easier everything would be if I wasn't here. If I didn't have to face my dad every day. How if I wasn't here I wouldn't feel the guilt over Mason's death. Because that guilt is tearing me apart.

The way Dad looks at me makes me want to be with Mason. He has to be in a better place now, because anywhere my father isn't would be better.

When we got home from the funeral, Dad was the worst I've ever seen him. No one knows what he's really like. He's always been so careful, but tonight I think he forgot I was there.

I'm so scared for her. I tried to protect her, and he hit me as well. Now I'm sitting in the treehouse with a bottle of bourbon, wishing I could climb in your window and tell you everything. Thinking about how much easier everything would be if I just disappeared, but wanting to say goodbye to you first, and then feeling guilty because I would be leaving Mum behind.

I can't leave her here on her own.

She needs me even more now that Mason is gone.

Now that he isn't here to protect both of us.

I have to protect her.

I hate my father.

I hate what he does to Mum.

I hate that my brother is dead.

I hate myself.

Levi.

Through blurry eyes I fold the letter closed. My heart hurts at what Levi has been through, and I sit staring at the box of letters on the floor in front of me. How many more has he written like this? How much pain and sorrow exists on these pieces of paper?

How am I supposed to help him?

How do I take his broken pieces and put them back together again?

My fight

Last night I stayed in the treehouse and read every single letter Levi wrote to me. I cried so many tears while on that platform in the trees, and it wasn't until Mum called my phone asking where I was that I realised how long I had been up there. When I'd gotten home and she had seen my puffy eyes, I'd explained them away as happy tears because I had finally spoken to Levi.

I'm not sure if she believed me.

This morning, I don't feel much better. I didn't get much sleep, and there's a hollow in my chest at the thought of talking to Levi about the letters today. There's someone else I want to talk to first though: Yvonne. I'm not sure how that's going to go.

"Are you going to the hospital again?" Mum asks.

"Yeah. I've made Levi a picnic basket. Figured hospital

food usually sucks, so I'd take him something nice."

"He hasn't been awake long," Mum says. "He might not be able to eat much."

"We'll see." I pick at the piece of toast in front of me. "Karen said she'd drive me in."

Mum smiles, then says, "We didn't get a chance to talk about uni last night."

I look up at her as she sips her coffee. "Can we not do this right now?"

"Well … I was going to say that I think you should do the course you have your heart set on." Mum smiles over the top of her mug.

I frown. "You don't want me to do law?"

Mum sighs. "I want you to be happy, Katie. And if that means doing a fine arts degree, then … I won't stop you."

"But I missed the interview. I'll have to wait until the mid-year intake."

Mum sets her coffee cup on the counter, and goes out to the dining room. She comes back with an envelope in her hand and passes it to me. It has the SCA logo in the top corner.

I rip it open to read the contents. As I scan the words, my mouth turns up into a smile and I jump up from the stool I've been sitting on at the counter.

"Thank you." I squeal and hug Mum.

She laughs. "You're welcome."

"How …?" I pull away and look at her.

"I emailed, and told them what you've been going through. They decided, due to extenuating circumstances, to allow you a reschedule date."

"Thank you," I say again.

Mum gives me another hug, then finishes her coffee. "I have a work thing this afternoon, so I'll see you tonight. Dad should be home this afternoon though."

"Okay." I watch her walk to the door then sit back at the counter.

I spend the next ten minutes in a state of happiness, staring into space as I finish my toast.

"Morning, space cadet," Daniel says from the other side of the counter.

I blink at my brother. "Hey."

"You looked like you were ..." Daniel waves his hand above his head, "somewhere else."

"Mum just gave me a letter from SCA. They've rescheduled my interview, so hopefully I haven't missed out on a place."

"That's great news," Daniel says. "How's Levi?"

Levi. I take a deep breath, because I'm not sure how to answer. My moment of happiness is gone as I think about what I need to talk to him about today. What I want to talk to Yvonne about, too.

"He's ... awake. And it's so great to hear his voice." I force a smile for my brother. "How's Jess after ... the other day?"

Daniel shrugs. "She's not great. I think Bridget has booked her into a psychologist."

"Oh," is all I manage to say. Then I think about all the stuff Levi wrote in his letters. "You have to promise me you'll do what you can for her. Look after her. Let her know that it's worth being here, and there are people who love her, even if she doesn't love herself right now."

"Wow, that was deep."

"I'm serious, Daniel." I stare at him. "Promise me you'll

tell her that."

"Yeah, I promise." He regards me for a moment. "What's happened, Katie? Did something happen?"

I shake my head. "It's okay. I just … I need to go and talk to Yvonne. I'll be back soon. Karen is taking me to the hospital." I get up and put my plate in the sink, then I hug my brother. "I love you."

He hugs me back. "I love you, too. Are you sure you're all right?"

"I'm good." I punch him on the arm then walk towards the front door. "I'll see you this afternoon. You'll pick me up, yeah?"

"Of course."

"You're the best."

"I know," he calls as I shut the front door.

I cross over through the garden to Levi's place, hoping Yvonne is still home and hasn't gone to the hospital yet. With a shaky hand, I knock on the door. Then I freak out because, seriously, what am I going to say? I go to turn around and leave when the front door to Levi's house opens.

"Katie?" Yvonne says. "How are you?"

"Hi." I give a pathetic little wave. "I … um … can … Is Mark home?"

Yvonne shakes her head. "No, sweetie. He went to work a couple of hours ago."

I take a deep breath. "Can I come in?"

"Of course." Yvonne steps aside and lets me through. "Would you like a drink?"

"Oh, no. I'm fine. Thank you." I follow her through to the kitchen, and it feels like an eternity since I've been inside Levi's house.

Yvonne sets two glasses on the kitchen bench anyway, and pours us both a glass of water from the jug beside the sink.

"Everything okay with you?" She raises a glass to her lips and takes a sip.

"I'm not sure. I mean … I'm all right. I just …" I sit at the counter and twist my fingers together. "I wanted to ask if you're okay?"

Yvonne smiles. "Yes, of course. I'm fine."

An uncomfortable quiet hangs between us, because we both know her words are a lie.

"I was in the treehouse again, the other night," I say.

"Oh, that's fine." Yvonne waves a hand. "You're welcome to go whenever you like."

"Thank you, but … I saw … I'm not sure what I saw. I just … he …" I stare at my hands. "I know Mark hits you."

Yvonne is silent for a few heartbeats, and I hold my breath. She's probably thinking, *what's this eighteen-year-old busybody doing in my house?* She's probably going to ask me to leave.

"Please don't worry about me, Katie," she finally says. "It was nothing."

"You know you can get help?" I say, not knowing if it's true or not. I've never experienced domestic violence before; I wouldn't know where to start. But there has to be some organisation or place she can turn to. Maybe even the police, if it came down to it. "And what about Levi? Has Mark … has he hit him, too?"

"Katie, really. We're fine."

I'm not sure what I expected her to tell me when I

thought coming over here was a good idea, but it's not okay. What her husband is doing to her is not acceptable.

I stand from the counter, anger at her calmness rising into my chest. "Did you know after Mason died, Levi thought about suicide? Did you know the only reason he's still here is because he wanted to protect you?" My voice gets louder at the last few words, and I clench my fists.

Yvonne's mouth drops open, then she closes it again. Her hand goes to her lips, and she squeezes her eyes closed. She takes a deep breath, then a big gulp of water from her glass.

"Did he tell you that?" She stares at me now, tears glistening in her eyes.

"Yes," I say, because even though Levi hasn't told me out loud, he wrote it in a letter. More than one, and I have to listen. I have to help him.

Yvonne presses her lips together. "I'll talk to Levi."

I nod, because what else can I say? Kick your husband out? I'm just a kid in her eyes. She's probably standing here thinking that she's the adult, and that I don't know anything.

A car horn sounds outside, and I look at my phone to check the time.

"Karen's here. I have to go. Thank you for the water." I turn to walk to the front door.

"Katie," Yvonne calls after me, and I face her again. "If you're going to the hospital now, he's been moved from the ICU."

"Thanks." I clutch my phone. "Are you going in?"

"I have some things to attend to this morning, but I'll be there this afternoon."

"Okay." I nod and turn back towards the door.

"Katie?" Yvonne says again when I put my hand on the doorknob. I face her. "I'm trying to … It's not easy after twenty years of marriage. I'm …" She pauses and attempts a smile. "Please don't worry. I'll sort it out."

I nod, and offer her a small smile. "I hope so."

And I do, because how can she be happy? How can Levi be happy having to live with what his father is doing to them?

When I get outside, I wave at Karen to wait while I run inside to grab my tote bag and the basket I put together for Levi. Seconds later the basket is on the back seat, I'm in the front with Karen, and we're driving to the hospital. The day I don't have to make this trip again will be a good one. I can't wait until Levi comes home so all I have to do is walk next door to see him.

"What's in the basket?" Karen asks.

"Nothing too exciting," I say. "Just something I put together for Levi."

Karen smirks, but doesn't push me to elaborate. She drops me off, and I tell her I'll see her later. Inside the hospital, I go to the front desk to ask where Levi is now.

"Up one floor then about halfway along," the nurse behind the desk says. "Room fifty-three."

"Thank you." I follow her instructions to Levi's room where I find the door open. I peek in, and he's not in his bed. The sheets are crumpled.

"Levi?" I call. "You here?"

I go into the room and set the basket on the table that slides up and down the bed. A toilet flushes, and the door to the adjoining bathroom opens. Levi comes out, dressed in his hospital gown and clutching his drip stand. He grins as he shuffles towards me.

I rush to him and take his arm. "Should you be up on your own?"

"I'm fine, Katie." He's shaky on his feet as I help him to the bed.

"What are you doing out of bed?" a nurse asks from behind us. "I told you to call me."

Levi chuckles. "And I told you I can manage on my own."

"Boys." The nurse shakes her head. "You haven't walked for a long time. I know you had physio every day while you were sedated, but it's not the same."

"You've told me this already." Levi sits on the edge of the bed and scoots back so he can swing his legs up.

"Slow and steady," the nurse says. She comes and takes his blood pressure and temperature, checks his drip, and writes something on his chart. "You need to keep an eye on this one." She smiles at me before leaving.

I look at Levi, and I can't help grinning. We grin at each other, and we must look like idiots, but I don't care. I'm so happy he's awake, and alive, and that we have another chance.

"What's in the basket?" he asks.

I tuck my hair behind my ears. "I brought you something."

I move the basket to the end of the bed, careful not to put it on Levi's feet, then move the table up the bed a bit so it's over his thighs. I go to the window and spin the rod so the venetians close a little. Then I flip the lid to the basket open and get to work.

Levi watches me in silence while I take out a small blue tablecloth and dress the hospital table. I line up five electric tea-light candles, because I figured the hospital wouldn't allow open flames, and then I set a bougainvillea clipping in the middle of the table. I glance at Levi from the corner of my eye, and he's still watching and smiling.

Next, I take out two wine glasses and a bottle of non-alcoholic champagne. Then I set down a plate and arrange some cheese, crackers, and dip. I pop the cork on the champagne bottle and fill the glasses, all while Levi doesn't say a word.

I pick up the glasses and hand one to Levi. "Cheers."

"Cheers," he replies.

We bump glasses before both taking a sip. The flavour is too sweet, and the bubbles shoot up my nose. I cough, then laugh.

"So …" I set my drink back on the table. "When can you get out of here?"

"I think I'm stuck for at least another week." Levi reaches out and pulls the table towards him, diving into the crackers and cheese. "The doctor said I'm not steady enough on my feet, and I need some more physio sessions before I can leave."

"How do you feel?" I ask, using a cracker to scoop up some dip.

"To be honest, really sore. My whole body aches."

"You were asleep for a while. I don't think you're going to feel perfect again overnight."

"I guess." He runs a hand through his hair, and my insides melt. "But enough about me. What's going on with you?"

"Oh, the usual," I say. "I read the letter you told me to … and the rest of them."

Levi raises his eyebrows. "You read all the letters?"

I sit on the edge of the bed with one leg under me. "Yeah, and I … There's something … I need …" I twist my fingers together in my lap and stare at them. This is harder than I thought it would be.

"You want to talk about the stuff I said," Levi says.

I chew on my lip and look at him. "You don't … you're not having those thoughts anymore, are you? Because I don't want you to go anywhere. Not after … you came so close to …" I stop again, because my throat is thick with emotion, and I have to hold my breath to stop the tears from coming.

Levi leans forward and takes my shaking hands in his. "I'm not thinking like that anymore."

I let out a long, shuddering breath and nod, because I still can't talk properly. And now I'm even more scared of the other thing I need to talk to him about. How do I tell him I saw his dad hit his mum? How do I ask him if he's being abused?

"Is everything …" I lick my lips. "Wow, I'm not doing so well with the talking thing today."

"It's okay." Levi squeezes my hands. "Take your time. I could tell you had a lot on your mind the minute I saw you today."

"I'm that transparent?"

"Like an open book."

"Okay," I say, then take yet another deep breath. "Your dad. I know everything is not okay between you and him, but … there's something I should tell you."

Levi rests back against his pillows. "What is it? Dad and I haven't gotten along for ages. From the letters, you should know what he's done to me."

"I'm more worried about what he's doing to your mum."

"Yeah, he treats her pretty badly."

"He hits her." I stare at him, and Levi looks at his hands. "He hits you." Saying the words out loud hurts more than I thought it would, but I can't even imagine what those words are doing to Levi. "Levi, look at me." He raises his head, and his eyes glisten with tears. "I'm not going to tell you what to do. I'm just worried about you, and … I'm not sure how to help other than talking to you about this."

Levi frowns and shrugs. "What's there to say?"

Now it's my turn to look away, because I'm not sure I can stare Levi in the face when I tell him what I need to. There's already too much pain in his eyes.

"The other day I was in the treehouse, and … I *saw* your dad hit your mum."

"What?" Levi's question comes out with a puff, and he sucks a deep breath back in.

"They came out to the back deck when I was in the treehouse, and I didn't mean to pry, or intrude, but I couldn't leave." I pick at a thread on the blanket on the bed. "I went to see your mum this morning."

"Why?" Levi asks.

"Because I'm worried about her." I look at him again. "I'm worried about you." We stare at each other for a few heartbeats, and it feels like a million years. The moment stretches out between us. "You have to … stop him somehow," I finally say.

Levi presses his lips together. "I'll talk to Mum. But I don't think it's going to help."

"Report him to the police."

"It's not that easy, Katie." Levi shoves both hands into his hair and pulls. "He's my dad."

"You shouldn't have to make excuses for him. You shouldn't have to protect your mum from him." My voice rises, and I stand from the bed. "You shouldn't be thinking about suicide."

"I'm not!" Levi says, his hands falling back to the bed with clenched fists.

"You should be able to feel safe in your own home," I say quietly.

"Katie is right," Yvonne says from the doorway, and I spin to face her.

"I'm sorry ... I—"

"Don't apologise." Yvonne holds her hand up. "You've given me the push I need to ..." She takes a deep breath. "To sort out ..." Yvonne swipes a tear from her cheek.

"Mum," Levi says, his face crumpling.

"I know, sweetie." She comes into the room and hugs her son.

Levi grips her tightly, and sobs into her chest. I back away towards the door, giving them some space.

"Katie, where are you going?" Levi asks, pulling away from Yvonne.

"You need to spend some time with your mum," I say, stopping in the doorway. "You've got a lot to talk about."

"Will you be back tomorrow?"

"Of course." I smile. "There's no chance of keeping me away."

He nods, and I give a nervous little wave before turning around and walking out to the corridor. I concentrate on putting one foot in front of the other, and I try not to think about how hard this is going to be for Levi. For Yvonne. I wish there was something I could do for them, but as much as I want to help, this time it isn't my fight.

12

Coming home

Over the next week I go to the hospital to see Levi every day. We spend our time talking mostly about the good stuff, and sometimes about the real issues that need to be talked about. Levi assures me his mum is taking steps to sort their shit out. I really hope it's true, because today he's coming home. And I'm a nervous wreck. I've spent the morning organising a surprise for Levi in the treehouse, and now I'm freaking out.

"What if he can't climb up there?" I say to Karen, twisting my fingers together. "He might not be able to climb the steps."

"I'm sure he'll be fine." She puts her hands on her hips, standing in the middle of my room. "Would you stop worrying?"

"It was a stupid idea," I say. "I shouldn't have done

anything."

"Oh my God, stop it," Karen says. "Stop fidgeting."

I clench my fingers and go to the window, kneeling on the window seat to stare out at the yard below. Yvonne told me she was picking Levi up late this morning. They should be home by now. I'm about to point this out to Karen when Yvonne's car pulls into the driveway.

I freeze.

What do I do?

Should I go down there? Or will he want to go inside first and get settled? He hasn't been home for a month and a half.

"What are you doing?" Karen asks.

I turn from the window and sit on the seat. "What if he doesn't—"

"Get up," Karen says. "Of course he'll want to see you."

When I don't move, she grabs my hand and yanks me to my feet. I follow her downstairs to the front door, catching a glimpse of Mum in the kitchen as we pass.

"Levi's home," Karen says as we go outside.

"That's great," Mum calls after us. "Say hi for me."

Before Levi is out of the car, Karen and I are standing on the lawn. Yvonne gets out of the front passenger side and comes around to the back passenger door on the driver's side. The trees in the driveway cast shadows over the window, so I can't see Levi's face. His mum opens the car door, and it's like everything happens in slow motion. I wait eagerly for Levi to stand, and when he does, I grin like an idiot. Yvonne helps him out and then leans into the back seat, coming out with a bouquet of flowers before closing the door. They're really pretty.

The driver's door opens, and Levi's dad gets out. He glances at Karen and me, a scowl on his face. I bite my lip. He slams the car door, looks at his wife and son, then turns and walks towards the front of the house.

I let out a breath I don't realise I've been holding.

Levi is walking, but his steps seem laboured and slow. He makes it to the front of the car, his gaze fixed on me. I wait for a few heartbeats before stepping through the garden to his side of the boundary.

My throat thickens, and I can't talk, even though I want to tell him how good it is to see him home. But I don't have to say anything, because Levi comes straight to me and wraps me up in a big hug.

"Hey, you," he whispers in my ear.

"Hey," I finally manage. "Welcome home."

He kisses the top of my head and rubs my back. "It's good to see you … here. Not in the hospital."

Yvonne places a hand on Levi's shoulder, and he pulls away from me slightly, keeping one arm around my waist. She passes him the bouquet of flowers, and he grips the base of the stems with one hand.

"I'll be inside." Yvonne pats Levi's arm.

He glances towards the house where his dad has stopped on the veranda. "I shouldn't be too long."

Yvonne smiles. "Take all the time you need."

My heart lurches as she walks towards the house and her abusive husband. I really hope what Levi told me about her trying to fix things is true. When she reaches the veranda, Mark holds the door open for her, but she doesn't look at him or speak to him.

"It's great to see you out of that bed," Karen says.

140

She's still standing in my front yard.

"You have no idea." Levi tightens his grip on my waist.

"Well … I'll let you catch up." Karen points to her mum's car. "I'm going to head."

"Can I ask a favour first?" Levi says.

I look between my best friend and my boyfriend, trying to guess what he wants, because I'm itching to take him to the treehouse. I also can't help wondering when he's going to give me the flowers.

"Sure," Karen says. "What's up?"

"I'm not really ready to, you know … drive myself anywhere," Levi says. "And Dad wouldn't stop on the way home. I'd rather go with Katie anyway. So I was wondering if …" He glances at me sideways. "I … um …"

"Spit it out." Karen laughs. "Where do you want me to take you?"

Levi looks at the flowers, then at his feet, then at Karen. "I want to go to … I want to …" He sighs. "The accident site. I haven't …"

"No problem," Karen says. "Get in." She heads towards the car.

I look up at Levi. "The flowers are for Josie?"

He bites his lip. "Oh God, I'm sorry. You thought they were for you?"

"No, don't be sorry," I say. "I think it's really nice … you wanting to go and see her … where … you know."

"The accident happened?" He kisses my temple. "Come on. I'm not sure I'll be able to go without you beside me."

I totally agree, so I don't say anything. The one time I went to the accident site with Karen was really, really hard. I haven't been back since.

Under Levi's insistence, I take the front passenger seat and he gets in the back. We take the back route from my place towards the highway, and the drive to where Josephine ran the stop sign takes less than five minutes.

Karen pulls over to the kerb before the intersection and kills the engine. The three of us sit in silence for a moment, and my heart hammers against my ribcage. From where we're stopped I can see the mass of tributes and flowers on and around the telegraph pole on the corner. I'm not sure I want to go and see it again.

But I'm not the one who wants to be here. Levi is, and he needs me.

I turn in my seat and look at him. "Ready?"

He picks up the bouquet of flowers from the seat beside him. "I guess."

"I'll wait here," Karen says.

I lick my lips and nod, then get out of the car. Levi joins me on the footpath, and we walk slowly towards the corner. It's as if neither of us wants to walk too fast because what we're walking towards is full of pain.

"I still don't remember that night," Levi says, stopping a few metres short of the telegraph pole.

"Maybe you don't need to." I slip my hand into his. "Maybe … what you need to remember is that forgiveness doesn't come easy, but it does come."

Levi squeezes my hand, and then he sucks in a sharp breath. When I look up at him, tears stain his cheeks. I swallow the lump in my throat, and gently pull him forward until we're standing at the base of the telegraph pole. Levi lets go of my hand and crouches, laying the flowers beside another fresh bouquet.

Josephine stares at us from the photo in the centre of the cross nailed to the telegraph pole. More letters, notes, photos, and flowers have been taped and tacked to the wood around it. They're different to the ones that were here when Karen and I came all those weeks ago. I wonder where they've gone, if someone collected them. They must have. Maybe Jessica has read some of them. If she has, I hope people's words have helped ease her pain.

I place a hand on Levi's shoulder as he stays crouched, his forearm resting on his thigh. He wipes his face with his other hand, then reaches out and touches a photo of Josephine with him, Jarred, Rachel, Veronica, and Geoff. It's the first time I've realised how much Josephine's death must be affecting them all. Like their group has been ripped down the middle.

Levi straightens and puts an arm around my shoulders. "Thank you." He pulls me close.

I'm not sure what he's thanking me for, so I just nod and press my cheek to his chest, wrapping my arms around his waist.

We head back to the car and Karen takes us home.

"I'll call you later," I say to her as I get out of the car.

"Whenever." Karen waves her hand.

Levi and I wait in the driveway until she pulls away and is driving down the street before turning back to each other.

"Now I can show you your surprise," I say.

"A surprise?" Levi raises his eyebrows.

I open my mouth to reply, but raised voices come from Levi's house, and my words die in my throat. We both stop and stare at his front door, waiting and listening. The shouts come again, and Levi rubs his face with his hands.

The front door bursts open, slamming against the wall of the house, and Yvonne comes out clutching her phone in her hand. She runs to the bottom of the steps.

"I'm not leaving," Mark yells, appearing in the doorway.

"Like hell you aren't." Yvonne turns and faces him. She looks so small standing at the base of the veranda steps. "I should've thrown you out a long time ago."

"This is my house." Mark points a finger at his wife.

"I will call the police," Yvonne yells, shaking her phone at Mark. "I'm not going to take any more shit from you."

Levi and I stand in my driveway, watching. I've never heard Yvonne raise her voice before, let alone swear. I have no idea what to do. I feel like if we move, they'll see us, but how can they not see us anyway?

"What … Should we do something?" I ask, pressing into Levi's side and gripping his hand.

Levi moves towards his yard, but his steps are laboured. When he lets go of my hand, my skin is cold, as if he's taken the memory of his touch with him. I follow close behind because I want to help, but I don't know how.

Mark moves down the steps, his face red and scrunched. "You'll do as I say and get inside the house."

"No." Yvonne stands her ground.

"Leave her alone," Levi says when he reaches his parents.

Mark's gaze flicks to Levi, then me, then back to his son. "Stay out of this, Levi."

He shakes his head. "No, Dad. I'm not going to let you hurt Mum anymore." Levi takes Yvonne's hand then positions himself between her and Mark. I stride over and stand with them, touching Yvonne's arm in a way I hope is reassuring.

"Get out of my way." Mark comes down the rest of the steps and grabs Levi, shoving him to the side.

Levi stumbles and falls, clipping the railing on his way down. He lands half on the path and half in the shrubs beside the steps.

"Levi!" Yvonne yells, reaching for her son.

I race forward to help Levi up. Mark lunges at Yvonne and grips her upper arms, throwing her up the stairs and onto the veranda. She cries out when she hits the wooden boards and bounces into the doorframe. Her phone skitters along the wooden surface.

"Mum!" Levi scrambles up the steps, but his movements are slow. "Don't touch her." He shoves his dad, but Mark is bigger than his son, and he hits back.

Levi stumbles. I reach the top step just as he misses it and falls past me, knocking me to the side. I turn to help him, but someone grabs my arm.

I face Mark. His fingers dig into my skin. "Let go of me," I yell, trying to yank my arm away. But he only grips me tighter.

"Let her go, you bastard." Levi pushes himself up and stands.

Mark drags me towards Yvonne and the door. I try to fight, but he's too strong. I struggle to look over my shoulder.

"Levi!"

"Katie!"

Levi makes it to the top step as Mark forces me into

the house. I stumble over Yvonne and fall into the foyer. Mark steps on his wife and comes into the house, turning his back to me. I run at him, but his big frame blocks the doorway as he leans down to grab Yvonne. *What the hell is this psycho doing?*

"Katie!" Levi calls my name again.

He reaches the door and grabs Yvonne's arm. She struggles in Mark's grip, and he and Levi use her like a tug-o-war rope. All the while Levi and Yvonne are yelling at Mark to let go. I can't get out through the blocked door. I can't reach Levi. I can't help Yvonne.

I can't do anything.

Mark twists and shoves Yvonne at me, and we both tumble onto the floor of the foyer.

"What are you doing?" Levi yells at his dad. "Let me in."

Mark doesn't reply. He grunts as he forces Levi back onto the veranda.

"Levi? Mark?" I hear Mum's voice. "Is everything okay?"

"Mum!" I scream, scrambling to my feet. "Mum!"

"Katie?"

I catch a glimpse of her as she reaches the top of the veranda steps, then Mark gives Levi a hard shove, sending him towards Mum, and slams the door, twisting the lock home.

The click echoes through the foyer.

"Levi!" Yvonne screams from behind me.

Levi pounds on the door. "Mum! Katie!"

Mark turns to face us, and I back away towards Yvonne who is standing at the bottom of the staircase. She grabs my arm and pulls me behind her, shielding me from

Mark. I quickly glance around. I haven't spent much time in this house over the past few years, but I still know it like the back of my hand. I thought I knew Levi's dad, too, but I guess not.

The only exits are the front door, the back door to the yard, and the glass sliding door upstairs to the deck. There are windows in the front lounge room big enough to climb out, but I can't see if they're unlocked.

"You need to get out," Yvonne says to Mark.

What do I do? I can't get past Mark to the back door, he's blocking the way. I have my phone in my back pocket, but I don't want to risk Mark seeing it.

Yvonne presses her back into me and it forces me onto the first step of the staircase. I stumble and fall onto the carpeted step with a thud.

"This is my house," Mark says. "I'm not leaving."

Yvonne takes a shuddery breath. "Then why don't we go and sit and have a drink."

"I don't want a drink." Mark lunges at Yvonne.

She tries to race up the stairs but falls on me. I should've gotten out of the way. Mark grabs her hand and pulls her off the steps.

"Stop," I say, trying to grab for her. "Please, stop."

Mark turns and backhands me across the cheek. My head whips to the side and hits the banister rail. Stars dance across my vision. I grip the wood to stop myself from falling.

"Run, Katie," Yvonne says, her voice a whisper.

I blink to clear my sight. Mark throws Yvonne to the floor and kicks her. Tears fill my eyes and spill over onto my cheeks, blurring my vision again. I scramble backwards then turn to climb the stairs. It's the only way I can go. When I reach the top I head straight to the door leading onto the deck. My hands are shaking so badly, I can't work the latch. I press my forehead to the cool glass and close my eyes, taking a deep breath.

The glass shudders and my eyes fly open.

"Katie!" Levi is standing on the other side. "Unlock the door."

His eyes go wide and he waves his hands, banging on the glass. I glance over my shoulder and Mark is coming towards me.

"Where are you going?" he asks, his voice low and gravelly.

A siren wails.

My heart explodes with panic as my fingers slide over the latch. *Why won't it open?*

"The other way," Levi yells. "Push it the other way."

I flick the lock, and a hand clamps down on my shoulder. Levi rips the door to the side. He grabs my hand and pulls me outside, slamming the sliding door closed onto Mark's arm. He grunts.

The sirens are louder.

Levi races towards the back steps that lead from the deck to the yard, his palm sweaty in mine. I have to concentrate on not tripping. I glance over my shoulder at the door and Mark turns the lock, pulling the curtains closed.

"Levi, your mum," I say when we reach the bottom of the stairs. "I think she's hurt."

"We called the police. Dad won't open the door." He pulls me along until we're in the front yard.

Two police cars are parked on the street, their lights flashing, and an ambulance is in the driveway. Mum and Dad are standing near the boundary, and when our gazes connect, I let go of Levi's hand and run to them. They both wrap their arms around me and smother me with their hugs.

"What happened?" Mum asks.

"Are you okay?" Dad pushes me to arm's length and looks me up and down, his eyes wide.

Levi reaches out to touch my forehead. "What did he do to you?"

"Your mum ..." My breath hitches. "They need to get inside."

"You're hurt, Katie," Dad says. "Can we get help over here, please?" he calls.

"I'm fine. Yvonne is the one who needs help."

An ambulance officer comes over to us. "Did you hit your head? Why don't you come and sit down?" She touches my arm.

"No," I say, moving away from her. "I don't want treatment. You need to get Yvonne out of the house. He ... he hurt her."

I look at Levi, and he has tears in his eyes.

"Katie," Dad says.

"Just get her out!" I yell, looking frantically from Dad to the police officers who are doing nothing but standing in the yard. "Get them to break the door down."

Mum grabs my hands and makes shushing noises. "It's okay, honey. I told them Mark and Yvonne's history. The police will get her out."

I frown. Levi runs a hand through his hair and grips

the back of his neck. He stares down at his feet. The lights from the police cars flash red and blue.

"You told … their history?" I stare at Mum. "You knew? You knew he was doing this to her? Why didn't you help her?"

"Katie." Levi grabs my arm. "Calm down."

I don't understand. I look from my parents to Levi, and then back again. If they knew, why didn't they do something? How could anyone let something like this happen?

Two police officers come over to us. They look too calm, like they're here for a cup of coffee. The male officer is tall and skinny, all angles. The female officer has short hair with tight curls.

"Hi. I'm Officer Beck and this is Officer Samson. Were you in the house?" the policewoman asks.

I nod. "But I'm fine—"

"How did you get out?"

"Back door," I say. "Up the top."

"Is he armed?" Officer Samson asks.

I shake my head. "No, but he's hurt Yvonne pretty bad."

"You need the ambulance officers to check you out," Beck says.

"I'm fine. You need to get Yvonne."

"Please. Go with the ambulance officer," Samson says. "We'll handle this."

They join two other police officers on the front veranda. They're just standing there though, and I want to scream at them to break the door down.

Levi turns me towards the ambulance in the driveway.

I go with the paramedic and sit on the open back of the ambulance. She shines a light in my eyes and checks me over, swabbing the cut on my forehead and putting a butterfly Band-Aid on it. I keep moving to look around her though, trying to see what's going on.

"Police. Open the door," one of the officers says, banging on the wood with a closed fist. "Mr White, you need to open up."

I hold my breath and will the door to open. Mark has to open the door. I'm not sure if he hurt Yvonne more after I ran. I squeeze my eyes closed, and the image of him kicking her fills my mind, so I open them again.

"Open the door," I whisper.

"I'll be back," Levi says, then jogs across the yard and up onto the veranda.

One of the policemen steps in front of him and says something. I can't hear their conversation. Levi puts his hands up, then points to the far corner of the veranda. The police officer goes in that direction, but I can't see what he's doing. When he comes back to Levi, he gestures for Levi to go down the steps.

"Mr White, we're coming in," one of the police officers says. "This is your last chance to open the door."

I stand from my seat on the tailgate of the ambulance and wrap my arms around myself. Levi comes back to my side.

"What's taking them so long?" I ask. "Your mum ..."

Levi puts his arm around my shoulders and pulls me close. "I know. It's okay, I told them where the spare key is."

"We're coming in," one of the police officers calls, and

the door to Levi's house finally opens.

Seconds later, an officer calls, "Can we get a paramedic in here now?"

Levi lets go of me and runs across the lawn. The two ambulance officers race after him to the house, medical cases in hand, and disappear through the front door. I feel helpless, unable to do anything but wait. All the police are inside. Levi is inside. Minutes pass and they feel like hours.

Mum and Dad come to stand with me near the ambulance. A few of the neighbours have come into the street, but they all seem to be keeping their distance. One of the paramedics comes back to the ambulance and gets a stretcher, rolling it to the bottom of the stairs.

Moments later, Yvonne comes out supported by Levi and the other paramedic. She's clutching her arm to her stomach, and blood covers one side of her face. She's helped onto the stretcher and rolled slowly to the ambulance. Levi walks beside her, clutching his mum's hand. Mum, Dad, and I step out of the paramedics' way.

"I'll go with her," Levi says, then he looks at me.

I nod and hug myself. "I'm fine. Go."

Levi climbs in beside his mum, heading for the one place he probably never wants to see again.

So much for coming home.

13

Our future starts now

They arrested Levi's dad.

The police brought Mark out of the house, handcuffed, not long after the ambulance took Yvonne away. They put him in the back of one of their cars, and I haven't seen him since.

Yvonne was treated for a fractured wrist, cuts, and severe bruising.

We all had to make statements.

They offered me a counsellor, but I told the police as long as Mark was never allowed near Yvonne and Levi again, I'd be fine.

That was four days ago.

Mum and Dad have been keeping a close eye on me. They think I haven't noticed, but they're acting as if I'm going to crack and fall apart at any moment. I won't. I don't think. They've even resorted to getting Daniel to suss me out whenever he can. He thinks I don't know what he's doing every time he asks if I'm okay.

Mark didn't hurt me as badly as he hurt Yvonne, but the look in his eyes and the memory of watching what he did to her will stay with me for a while.

The police put out a temporary restraining order on Mark so he's not allowed to go near Yvonne, at least until it goes through court properly. I might have to testify, especially since Mum and Dad want to press charges for what he did to me. I don't know what's going to happen there though. I guess we have to wait and see.

I'm not sure what any of it means for Levi. I know it's not the end of it for him or his mum, but at least it's a step towards getting Mark out of their lives. I'm still so angry at myself for never realising what was happening to them.

After Levi had come home, Mum offered for him to stay with us, since Yvonne was in hospital. I'd wanted to take him to the treehouse, but with everything that had happened, the surprise I'd planned didn't seem so important anymore. Instead, we'd spent half the night out in my back yard, lying on the grass and staring at the stars. The lights from the marina down the hill had been winking, and we'd talked about the time we bashed through the bush all the way down to the road at the bottom, then walked to the ferry.

We don't do that this time though. We take Mum's car and drive down the windy road, parking on our side of the river, before jumping on the ferry to go across to the marina. Being on the ferry on foot is so much better than sitting in the car. It's as if the trip goes in slow motion, and there's more of a chance to take it all in. The grinding of the gears as the cable feeds through the pulleys. The dark water beneath us. The feeling of moving while standing still.

When we reach the other side, Levi and I sit on the wall beside the boat ramp, our toes dipping into the coolness below. I rest my head on his shoulder, and let the warmth of the sun soak my face. The water from the river laps against the shore to our left, and jostles the boats in their pens to our right.

I haven't come down here since we were kids.

I miss it.

There's something about the sound of the water, and the birds in the surrounding bush mixed with the low hum of voices from the marina café, that's soothing.

"We should do this more often," I say, with my eyes closed and my face tilted to the sky.

Levi rests his head against mine. "We can do this as much as you like."

I don't open my eyes, but I know he's smiling. I can hear it in his voice.

"Did you sort uni out?" I ask.

"I'm going to do mid-year intake. So until then, I'm free." He laughs.

I chuckle and straighten up so I can look at him. "I can't believe I have to start in a few weeks. I feel like this summer has disappeared, and we didn't get …" I stop because my voice starts to shake, and a lump rises into my throat. I stare out at the water, looking for a way to say all the things I want to say but can never find the right words.

Levi nudges my shoulder. "Everything will work out."

I turn back to him and he puts his arm around my shoulders, pulling me closer for a kiss. His lips are soft and gentle, and I never realised how much I missed him while he was in hospital. Missed the way his lips would curl when he smiled at me. Missed how when he ran his hand through his hair it made my belly flop. Every time I hear the sound of his voice, and feel the beat of his heart under my fingertips, I'm so scared it will be the last time that it makes me want to cry.

I pull away and press my palm to his chest. "We have so much hanging over our heads."

Levi puts a finger to my lips. "The past is done with, okay?"

I nod, unable to speak because the lump in my throat is still there.

My phone buzzes in my back pocket, but I ignore it. I know it's going to be Karen, and I hope she's finished with what I asked her to do, but I can't check because I don't want Levi to read the text message over my shoulder.

"We can still see your house from here." I point to the top of the hill across the river.

Levi looks up at the bushland. "Dad always made sure the trees were cut back enough not to lose the view." He smiles, but then it falters.

We go silent, and my heart lurches. I hope that it's not always going to be like this. That at some point in the future we'll be able to talk about him and not have it hurt. But that time isn't now. My dad never worried about the view, and I like that I know my house is there, too. It's hidden behind the screen of bush.

"Want to go back and look at the view?" I ask.

"If you're with me, I don't care where we are." Levi gets up and stands so his toes hang over the edge of the wall. He holds his hand out to me and I take it, letting him help me to my feet. He pulls me close and I shut my eyes, savouring the feeling of his arms around me, the sunlight on my skin, and the calmness I feel being here with him.

We put our thongs on, then walk slowly back towards the ferry, hand in hand. My phone buzzes again, and this time I take it out to read the messages. I pull my hand from Levi's and cup it around the screen so he can't see.

Karen: All set. Treehouse ready n waiting

Karen: When r u home?

Karen: UR obvs having 2much fun!

Karen: Going 2 C Jess

I smile at her words, but my heart lurches a little at the mention of Jessica. She's still not doing so well, and I'm grateful now that she has Daniel. The idea of my brother being with one of my closest friends has grown on me, and I figure if he can help her through the pain, then that's a good thing.

I flick Karen a quick reply.

Me: Heading 2 ferry now. Thnk you. C U 2morrow?

Karen: Of course

"Let me guess," Levi says. "Karen?"

I smirk and pocket my phone. "Who else? But you have my undivided attention now." I slip my arm around his waist and tuck myself into his side as we walk the last twenty metres to the ferry.

It's on its way back across the river, so we have to wait a few minutes before we can board. I lean against the railing overlooking the water and stare into the depths below. It's like thinking about the future. I've no idea what lies beneath the surface of the inky water, just like I don't know what lies ahead of me. The thought scares me, and I worry that something terrifying will launch itself out of the darkness. I've survived so much already. Levi has, too. If we can make it through all the days that have led us to this point, then we can make it through many, many more.

"You okay?" Levi asks. "You're quiet, and staring into space."

"Yeah." I smile, looking up at him. "Just thinking."

I don't know what the future holds, and as scary as it might be, I have to remind myself that at least now Levi and I have a chance at a future together. At least now I know I have him, and we have to make the most of every second, because no one knows when everything will end.

The ferry grates along the concrete as the ramp slides up, and it comes to a stop. The ferry master runs out and presses the button for the boom gate to let the cars off. We walk onto the ferry along the pedestrian path and stop about halfway, leaning against the railing. I stare out across the water, standing beside Levi so our shoulders are touching.

We don't talk for the ten minutes it takes the ferry to get to the other side. We just stand there, letting the breeze play with our hair, and enjoy the quiet and peace of the river.

I drive us back up the hill towards home. Levi isn't comfortable getting behind the wheel of a car. His BMW was a complete write-off. Even though he can't remember what happened on the night of the accident, I think guilt over Josephine's death still plagues him.

I pull Mum's car into the driveway and turn the engine off, nervous about what's going to happen next. When my surprise for Levi fell through on the day he came home from hospital, I never thought I'd have another chance to pull it off. Considering the treehouse is in his backyard, it was going to be hard to go out there without him noticing or seeing me.

That's where Karen came in, and I hope she did a good job.

This time it's going to be a surprise for both of us.

"I have something to show you," I say, curling my fingers through the door handle.

Levi opens the car door and sticks one leg out. "Really? What is it?"

I smile. "If I told you, it wouldn't be a surprise."

We get out of the car, and my chest tightens. I break out in a light sweat, nervous and shy, and suddenly worried this is stupid. What if Levi thinks it's a bad idea? What if what I want him to do is too much for him?

Get a grip, Katie. It's just paper.

And he told me the past was done with.

I meet Levi at the front of the car. "It's in the treehouse." I fidget with the car keys. "Think you can climb the steps?"

"For you, I could climb a mountain with two broken legs."

"I'm serious." I swat him on the arm. "I don't want you to hurt yourself. You're not supposed to be overdoing it."

"I'll be fine." Levi gently takes my hand and we walk towards the side of the house.

His steps are slower than usual, and cautious, as if he's done too much today, and I have doubts about him being able to make the climb. But he says he can, so I'm not going to stop him. When we reach the bottom of the tree, Levi looks down at me.

"It's been a while since we've both been up there ... together," he says.

"It has." I smile, and remember when Levi chose truth at Veronica's party. We were always innocent in this treehouse. Maybe that will change today. "You first." I gesture to the pieces of wood nailed to the trunk that make the steps.

Levi sets one foot on the bottom piece of wood and grabs another with his hands. Slowly, he works his way up, and when he reaches the top he stops with the edge of the platform at his waist. At first I think he's stopped because he can't go any farther, but then he glances down at me, his eyes wide.

"Katie, this is amazing," he says. "When did you do this?"

"A good witch never reveals her secrets." I chuckle. "Now get in so I can come up, too." My smile widens, and my cheeks hurt. I'm not about to admit I have no idea what it looks like in there.

Levi pulls himself up the rest of the way and I follow. At the top I sit on the edge of the platform and swing my legs onto the wooden floor. I have to hold in my gasp. When

I told Karen romantic, I never thought she'd go this far.

Levi is sitting on the table in the corner, gazing around at the fairy lights strung up across the two walls, the tea lights set at regular intervals around the edge of the floor, and the bougainvillea flowers scattered around.

"Did you get new curtains?" Levi asks.

"Yep." I shuffle away from the edge of the platform. "The old ones were a bit gross."

"They're great." He reaches out and touches the bright purple fabric. "It's all great, Katie."

"Look under the table." My voice shakes a little, and I hope Levi doesn't notice.

He raises his eyebrows but does as he's told. He pulls out the box of letters, and a mixing bowl. The lighter I put inside the bowl moves, scraping against the metal sides.

"What's this for?" He holds the box in one hand and the bowl in the other.

I take a deep breath and close my eyes for a second, hoping that when I say what I want to say, he'll agree with me.

"That box ... everything in it is in the past. It's full of pretty sucky memories for both of us, and I'm not sure about you, but I'm done with all of that. I want to move forward with nothing hanging over my head. I want to put all that stuff behind me. Behind us, and start from now." I stare into Levi's eyes and smile. "I don't want to waste another minute, because you ... you're my everything, and ..." I can't keep talking because a sob rises into my chest.

Levi gets off the table, sets the box and bowl down, and kneels in front of me. "I know," he whispers, and then he kisses me, my tears falling onto our lips.

Levi pulls away and sits back on his heels. He sets the bowl between us and picks up the lighter. Then he opens the shoe box and grabs a handful of the letters, putting them into the bowl. He strikes the flint and holds the flame to the corner of the envelope sitting on top.

The fire spreads quickly, and we stare into the flames. They flicker between us, and as the pile crumples, Levi feeds more letters into the bowl until all of them are nothing but pieces of black, wispy ash.

He looks at me and smiles. "I love you, Katherine Sullivan."

Another tear rolls down my cheek. "I love you, too, Levi White."

He reaches out and wipes my tears away. The rough skin of his fingers anchors me in the present, and I press my cheek into his palm. We've been through so much, and come so far, from when I thought Levi and I had something, to when he made me feel like nothing, and back to him being my everything.

We've come out the other side together.

The past is where it should be … in the past.

Our future starts now.

The end

Acknowledgements

I feel like I've already thanked everyone I need to with this series, because they've been written one after the other. It's as if I wrote the three parts as one long book. But I need to mention the most important people who have helped me through every stage.

Selina Fenech and Serene Conneeley, thank you for the encouragement, for pushing me when I needed it, and for letting me whinge when I needed it, too. Writing can be a lonely profession, but having both of you around makes it so much better. I just might keep you, if that's okay.

To my family, as always, thank you for your endless love and support.

Thank you to the Story Queens. I couldn't ask for a better group of writers and friends. Each of you has supported me in different ways, and I'll be forever grateful for the influence you've had on my writing journey.

Lauren Clarke, editor extraordinaire … thank you so much for all the time and effort you put into my manuscripts. My words would be shadows of themselves without you.

Finally, to my readers, I hope Katie's story touched your heart, and I'd like to thank you for sticking with her and Levi until the end.

About the author

K. A. Last was born in Subiaco, Western Australia, and moved to Sydney when she was eight. Artistic and creative by nature, she studied Graphic Design and graduated with an Advanced Diploma. After marrying her high school sweetheart, she concentrated on her career before settling into family life. Blessed with a vivid imagination, K. A. Last began writing to let off creative steam, and fell in love with it. She is currently studying her Bachelor of Arts at Charles Sturt University, with a major in English, and minors in Children's Literature, Art History, and Visual Culture. She now resides in the countryside on the mid-north coast of NSW with her family and a menagerie of animals.

Connect with K. A. Last

Website www.kalastbooks.com.au
Facebook www.facebook.com/KALastBooks
Instagram www.instagram.com/kalastbooks
Pinterest www.pinterest.com/kalast
Goodreads www.goodreads.com/KALast
Twitter www.twitter.com/KALastBooks

**Scan the code to subscribe to
K. A. Last's newsletter.**

Available Now

Is love really worth the fall?

THE TATE CHRONICLES

Scan for more information